Surviving ADAM MEADE

Shannon Klare

Swoon
READS
Swoon Reads New York

A SWOON READS BOOK

An imprint of Feiwel and Friends and Macmillan Publishing Group, LLC
175 Fifth Avenue, New York, NY 10010

Our books may be purchased in bulk for promotional, educational,
or business use. Please contact your local bookseller or the Macmillan
Corporate and Premium Sales Department at (800) 221-7945 ext. 5442
or by e-mail at MacmillanSpecialMarkets@macmillan.com.

Library of Congress Cataloging-in-Publication Data
Names: Klare, Shannon, author.
Title: Surviving Adam Meade / Shannon Klare.
Description: First edition. | New York : Swoon Reads, 2018. | Summary:
At first unhappy about transferring to a new high school senior year, Claire
quickly makes friends and, despite her determination to avoid football,
captures the attention of the arrogant quarterback.
Identifiers: LCCN 2017041922 | ISBN 9781250154378 (hardcover) |
ISBN 9781250154361 (ebook)
Subjects: | CYAC: Football—Fiction. | Dating (Social customs)—Fiction. |
High schools—Fiction. | Schools—Fiction. | Family life—North
Carolina—Fiction. | North Carolina—Fiction.
Classification: LCC PZ7.1.K634 Sur 2018 | DDC [Fic]—dc23
LC record available at https://lccn.loc.gov/2017041922

Book design by Danielle Mazzella di Bosco

First edition, 2018

1 3 5 7 9 10 8 6 4 2

swoonreads.com

To Mom and Dad
for teaching me to go after my dreams.

And to Allen
for all those late nights along the way.

Water Girl

I should've negotiated better.

My shoulders burned beneath the North Carolina sun, the heat contrasting cold water at my feet. Mud stirred beneath my tennis shoes, soaking the black mesh fabric. I was supposed to be today's team manager, but I was more like a muck-covered version of Cinderella.

"Claire, we need those!" my dad called.

I lifted my attention and spotted him walking down the sideline, pointing at a pair of water bottles thrown near the field. Great, now there were two more bottles to fill. Yay. Perfect. Exactly what I hoped.

"Get them in a sec," I answered, annoyed by the never-ending water bottle shortage.

A whistle blew, stopping all movement on the field. Third

water break in an hour. It was like my dad wanted me to be miserable.

My pulse quickened as football players, their jerseys soaked with sweat, swarmed the water like mosquitoes. A hulking lineman snatched the water hose from me and let the water flow across his tanned chin. He smelled like onions and dirt, a stench strong enough to make my eyes water. This was a million times worse than the usual crusty-gym-shorts-and-soggy-cleats scent my brother, Case, wore. And the lineman wasn't the only one. I was surrounded by a crowd of guys who smelled like butt.

I tried to filter my breathing through the damp collar of my T-shirt, but there was nowhere to breathe. I could taste their odor on my tongue, drowning me with no escape.

"Claire!" my dad hollered, his voice carrying across the field. Silver keys glistened in his hand.

Oh, thank goodness. I jogged across the grass, sweat beading my forehead as I stopped in front of him. Without hesitating, I reached for the keys.

"Not so fast," he said, raising them out of reach. "I haven't told you what I need."

"Let me guess," I answered, sighing as I put my hands on my hips. "More water bottles? Towels? Air freshener for your team of guys with foul-smelling pits?"

"How did you know?!"

I glared at him, and he laughed, his teeth flashing white against tanned skin. He'd be a warm golden brown by the end of the day, and I'd look like a strawberry. Unfortunately, the tanning genes weren't ones I inherited.

"Wow," he said, maintaining a grin. "You look *just* like your mom when you do that."

"I look like Mom ninety percent of the time." I glanced at the keys again, then him. "Can I go now?"

"For a little bit," he answered. "It's your lunch break. Grab some food, don't wreck my truck, and we'll discuss the terms of our negotiation when you get back."

He handed me the keys. I took them gladly.

"The terms were already negotiated," I reminded him, spinning the key ring on my finger. "Two days grueling manual labor in exchange for a weekend trip to Baker Heights. We shook on it. It's too late to change your mind."

"We'll see."

No. There wasn't a *we'll see*. I needed a trip home like I needed air. This was a matter of survival—social survival. One way or another, I was going to Baker Heights.

"You'd better hurry before they empty all the water bottles," he commented, deflecting my attention.

"They keep flying through water bottles, and you'll be at the next city council meeting explaining how those guys drank the town out of water," I answered.

"Pader is small, but I'm pretty sure there's enough water to last us a practice," he said.

"Well, I hope you're wrong."

His mouth twitched at the corners. "If I'm wrong, I'll blame you for wasting all that high-quality h-two-o."

"You'd throw your daughter under the bus? Thanks, Dad."

"Anytime." He chuckled and pointed at a gap in the fence. My exit. "You should head out," he said. "Can't promise you'll get another opportunity to grab food. You're cranky when you're hungry."

"That's a personality trait I got from you."

"Really?" He tilted his head, the crinkled corners of his eyes barely visible beneath dark sunglasses. "Fine," he answered. "No lunch for you."

"No!" I tucked the keys into my pocket for safekeeping. "I have to get away from here. Those guys reek. We're talking a five-out-of-five odor ranking. I'm nauseous just thinking about it."

He looked at the sideline. "They can't smell any worse than your brother."

"Oh, but they do," I answered.

My eyes narrowed as I glanced at the sweaty team. Most of them were squirting the contents of my freshly filled water bottles on their heads. All my hard work was going down the drain, again.

"That's why there's water everywhere," I said. "Could you tell them this isn't a shampoo commercial? The water should be in their mouths, not on their heads."

"To be fair, it's hot out."

"Does it look like I'm concerned with the temperature?"

He frowned at me, but I ignored him. The summer heat didn't give them an excuse to waste water, or my time.

"That's a little inconsiderate," he said.

"Doesn't mean it isn't true," I answered. I tapped my tennis shoe against the grass. It squished from the water soaked through my soles. "And I'm not the only one who's inconsiderate. One of your linemen stole the water hose from me. He was lucky he didn't get bit."

"Football players never bugged you before."

"Because I used to like them," I answered. His face softened, and I looked away. "I don't want to talk about football players. I want to suffer through this practice, get my trip home, and be done."

"You could try looking on the bright side of things," he said. I stared at him, confused, and he shrugged. "This is grade-A bonding time with your dad."

"I'd rather be home watching TV." I turned, spotting the opening in the fence. "I'm going to lunch. I'll be back around one."

"You can break until one thirty," he replied, "but grab sunblock. I don't want your mom griping at me when you come home sunburned. While you're out, you can also grab a Pader High hat from my office. Should keep the sun off your face."

"I hate hats," I groaned.

"I hate getting in trouble with your mom." He blew the whistle, and I jumped at its shrill cry. "Grab the hat and contribute to my happiness. Okay?"

"Give me your credit card and contribute to *my* happiness," I replied.

"Uh, wasn't born yesterday." He pointed a wooden clipboard in the direction of the tackling dummies. The players dropped the water bottles and sprinted across the field. "I need to get out there. Take the hat and be thankful."

"I have a Baker Heights hat at the house. I'll grab that one instead."

His smiled faded to a frown. "Don't be difficult, please."

"I'm not, but I'm not wearing a Pader High hat, either."

He shook his head, his shoulders stiff as he crossed the field. He could be frustrated with me, but I still had a point.

Truth was, I should've been in Baker Heights, enjoying the remainder of my summer and looking forward to my last year of high school. I was supposed to be on the lake, waterskiing and slumming it up with my friends. Yet here I was—football team flunky for the day. I left practice, headed for the field house two streets over. The smell of freshly cut grass hung in the air outside the high school, while echoes of the football team mixed with the slam of car doors. Teachers hauled boxes into the school, prepping for the students' return. Week one would be here soon enough. The realization made my pulse race. This wasn't my first time at a new school, but senior year wasn't the time to start over. I wasn't ready to endure the dreaded new-girl effect, when I didn't want to be here in the first place.

"Hey, water girl!" a guy said, his voice coming from the direction of the field.

Confused, I turned. I wasn't the water girl, but I was the only non–faculty member outside the school.

Outfitted in white practice pants and a telltale red jersey, a football player jogged across the road. Red meant one thing— quarterback status. Despite his helmet-hidden face, I knew his name. Adam Meade. Pader High's quarterback extraordinaire. He was my dad's constant conversation topic, the player colleges were always calling about, and what I understood to be the best thing since sliced bread.

I motioned at myself as Adam stopped in front of me. "I'm Claire. I'm not the water girl."

"You get the water, therefore you're the water girl." He handed me a key and nodded toward the field house. "Coach wants you to bring the Gator when you come back. You need that to turn it on."

"Did he say why he needs it?" I asked, spotting the sports vehicle parked beside the field house.

"Nope. He just said he needs you to bring it."

I pocketed the key, and Adam shifted the weight on his feet, his light eyes surveying me from behind the metal facemask.

"Does he need anything else?" I asked.

"He doesn't. I do." I quirked an eyebrow, and Adam shrugged. "We need ice. The last water girl was always good about bringing a cooler to the field, but there isn't one out there. Get on her level, or you'll be replaced."

Replaced?! I stared at him, my blood boiling. I wouldn't bring him ice. I'd bring him a special water bottle filled with the tears of my enemies.

He turned and jogged back to the field, leaving me dumbfounded as I tried to pull my jaw from the ground. Adam may be the quarterback, but I wasn't a pushover. If he wanted to piss me off, he could deal with the consequences.

* * *

"You're a sight for sore eyes."

A cool breeze swept across my mom's floral shop, carrying the smell of fresh paint and cardboard boxes. Being inside was a welcome change, but the longer I stood beneath the air-conditioner vents the more I dreaded going back to the field.

My mom moved behind the counter, her dark hair tossed into a messy ponytail and her gray T-shirt damp with sweat. The bags under her eyes and streaks of dust on her cheeks told me one thing—she was exhausted. She worked long hours trying to get this place ready to open, and it looked like she was finally making progress.

"You've gotten a lot done," I said.

She leaned against the counter and smiled. "Been here since

seven. Finished painting, then started on the candle display. What do you think?"

I glanced at the long row of narrow wooden shelves near the door. They were filled floor-to-ceiling with cylindrical candles of every variety and looked like every other candle display. It wasn't bad. Mediocre.

"I like it if you like it," I told her, forcing a smile as I pushed a wayward strand of hair behind my ear. "Speaking of what I like, I'd like to borrow the car when I go to Baker Heights."

"You share the car with Case," she replied. "You need to talk to him about taking it to another state."

"But I'm the oldest! I'm immune from asking Case to borrow anything."

"Sorry. That's not how life works." She grabbed a box from the floor and hauled it onto the counter. "Will you put that up?" she asked, pointing at a vase near the register. "There's a spot over there where it'll be safe."

Vase in hand, I sulked to the far wall where the rest of the vases sat. "Can't we skip the sibling rules for once?" I said. "You purchased the car. You have final say."

She pulled a set of gift tags from the box and placed them on the counter. "If I give you permission without mentioning it to him, he'll say I played favorites. I'm not getting stuck in the middle."

"Stupid little brothers."

"You'd do the same thing." She slid the tags toward the register and lifted her gaze. "What time are you supposed to be back at practice? I doubt you're done for the day."

"One thirty," I answered.

"And how is it going?"

"Awful. The guys smell so bad flies won't even go near them."
I faked a gag, and she grinned. "Any cute ones that don't smell bad?"

"Nope." I returned to the counter and leaned against it, arms crossed. "And it doesn't really matter if they're cute. Football players are off my radar. Remember?"

"You've spent two days at the field. I thought you might have changed your mind."

"My mind isn't changing," I answered. "After today, I'm done. No Friday night games. No pep rallies. Nothing."

"What about cheerleading?"

"Nothing," I repeated. "I plan on spending the season at home. We're talking Friday nights full of reality shows and food. Who knows, maybe I'll decide to toss on a mud mask and paint my nails. The goal is total relaxation. If you want to skip the games, you're more than welcome to join me."

"I can't do that, and you won't either," she argued. "Football is in your blood. Pretending you don't care won't make it go away. Watch. You'll be on the sidelines of every game, and I'll be there to say I told you so."

"It isn't going to happen."

Her grin faded. I knew what she was thinking, and I didn't feel like having that conversation again. Once was more than enough.

"I need to head out," I said. "If I'm late, Dad will give me a more annoying job than water girl. Which, by the way, is the worst job on the planet."

"You used to like filling bottles."

"I used to like a lot of things." My chest tightened, and I swallowed emotions swelling in my throat. "I've got to go."

"Claire."

I reached the door but didn't make it all the way through before my mom said, "Give Pader a fair shot, and you can borrow the car for your trip to Baker Heights."

"Excuse me?" I shifted my gaze to her, meeting eyes the same shade of blue as mine. "What do you mean give it a fair shot?"

"I mean get involved," she answered. "Be nice to people. Find friends. You don't have to love it here, but give it a try."

"And I'll get a car for my efforts?"

"You'll get the car for your trip," she said. "Fair?"

I crossed the shop and stopped in front of the counter. I couldn't promise to be prom queen, but I could force a smile and fake it until my mom believed it was real.

"I'll try to like this place, and you'll let me borrow the car," I said, shaking her hand. "You've got yourself a deal."

Itching for War

"This sucks."

Freshly waxed tile squeaked beneath my tennis shoes, muffled by banging locker doors and voices of students I didn't know. All morning I'd been a fish in a fishbowl, stared at and wondered about. It was the dreaded new-girl effect, but I was over it. The day couldn't end soon enough.

I sipped from a water bottle as I searched for Case's locker in Junior Hall. Today would've marked the first day of my final year at Baker Heights. My friends would be walking the halls with me, talking about cheer practice or making plans to hit Sonic after school. Seth would be there, too.

Seth. I sucked in a breath and tried to swallow the knot in my throat.

Where was Case? I scanned the hallway for my little brother. Before I could find him, someone backed into me. A backpack collided with my hand, and my water bottle splashed to the floor.

"Sorry, sweetheart," a guy said, flashing me a smile as he backed away.

He was taller than Case, maybe six one or six two, with light eyes, dark hair, and a perfect face. He continued down the hall, chatting with a blond girl instead of helping me with the mess.

"I was drinking that!" I said. "But it's cool. The tile looked like it needed it more than I did."

The guy gave me a thumbs-up over his shoulder and carried on.

"Jerk," I grumbled.

"Saw what you did there," Case said, coming to a stop beside me. "Congrats. Your comebacks are the stuff of legends."

"I'm already mad. Drop the sarcasm, okay?" I grabbed the water bottle and hurled it into the nearest trash can.

"That's the I'm-gonna-hurt-someone walk," Case said, following me through the hall. "Should I go to class or stay here and reel in your attitude?"

"My attitude isn't my fault."

"Right."

"It's not." I pointed at the idiot in front of us. "Blame that guy. He just left the mess. Didn't even get me a paper towel. What happens when someone falls in the puddle and breaks their leg? That's on me."

"Tell a janitor," Case answered. I scowled at him. "Okay, I'll tell a janitor."

"Thanks." I searched for the cafeteria entrance and came up empty. "I don't know about this," I said, giving up. "These people are rude, and I don't like this school. I want to go home."

Case positioned himself in front of me. He was a massive roadblock in a graphic tee and faded jeans. "Okay," he answered. "First off, you *are* home. Second, you don't like this school because you don't know it. Third, these people are nice." He gave a high five to a passing guy and shot me a pointed look. "See. Making friends already."

"Yeah, because you're an athlete and a guy. It's easier for you."

"It would be easy for you, too, if you'd try."

"I am trying." He pursed his lips, and I rubbed the back of my neck. "Okay, that was a lie," I said. "I just don't see the point. It's my last year of high school. Why waste the effort?"

"Because it's worth the effort."

"For you," I said. "You've got another year here, unless Dad decides to take a different job. Who knows, maybe you'll get to start over your senior year, too."

The bell rang, and Case glanced at the clock beside the library. "Great," he muttered. "I'm late. This is your fault."

"Well, you always make *me* late. It's time I returned the favor."

"I don't make you late."

"Right." I nodded. "You just take forty-five-minute showers and use all the hot water."

"Got to get my luscious locks fully conditioned," he answered, raking a hand through his brown hair. "It takes time."

"Well, you and your luscious locks are about to miss fifth period. Dad's going to be pissed when I tell him."

"You shouldn't threaten people who know where you sleep," he said, frowning as he shifted his weight.

"I'm not worried. I know how long you wet the bed."

Case darted a glance around the hall, panic on his face. "You can't blurt out things like that. I have a rep to keep."

"My bad. Forgot you were trying to be cool."

"I'm not trying to be cool," he said. "I *am* cool."

Case hurried off, and I continued searching for the cafeteria. Five minutes later, with a tray in hand, I plopped into a plastic chair at an empty table. Beneath bright fluorescent lights and laminated posters, most of the students were clustered randomly. The football players were an exception. Their table was all guys, with the exception of a blond girl. She sat across from the same guy who made me drop my water, laughing with him and a few others.

I popped a french fry in my mouth and watched them. She looked at ease with the players, like she was one of them, and the sight tugged at memories I tried to bury. I was like her once, an honorary member of the team. Even before Seth, before I was dating one of them, Baker Heights' football team had welcomed me in. Now I was just a new girl. I was the one people stared at and whispered about. I was alone.

I pulled my phone from my pocket and tried to find a distraction. I found it in pictures from the spring, pictures of Seth and me.

His dark brown eyes were caring then, warm as he looked at me. His smile was carefree, his body relaxed, and his overgrown brown hair tousled by the breeze. Things had changed between us, but the guy I knew had to be in there somewhere. I needed that guy now. I needed to talk to him.

For the first time in months, I texted him.

Claire: I miss you

The bell rang, and the room became a frenzy as students stood, discarded their trays, and filed out of the cafeteria like a herd of cattle, bound for another three periods before freedom arrived. I filed out with the rest of them, entering a hallway where the smell of burned chicken sandwiches and stale fries lingered.

Closer to Senior Hall, that smell faded. The metallic scent of lockers and the sugar-cookie aroma from home economics took over instead.

My locker was beside Mrs. Myers's math class, nestled among college posters, school memorabilia, and inspirational quotes. Most of the morning, students entering and exiting math blocked my way. This time, it was the guy who made me drop my water bottle. I sidestepped a group of people and stopped behind him, his fitted blue T-shirt, dark jeans, and messy brown hair familiar for all the wrong reasons.

"Excuse me," I said, my tone the nicest I could manage. "Can I get by?"

He ignored me.

"Hello? Excuse me," I said, trying again. When he failed to acknowledge me for the second time, I reached up and tapped him on the shoulder. "Yo. You with the hair and inability to hear."

The person he was talking to, a shorter guy with brown eyes, olive skin, and curly black hair, craned his head my way. I stared at him and pointed at the idiot in front of me.

"Adam, I think she needs you," he said.

Adam turned, the angular planes of his face tight with annoyance. He was annoyed with me? No. Not after the water girl incident *and* the water bottle mishap.

Light green eyes, framed by thick lashes, peered at me. "They all need me," he said, addressing his friend, "and she can wait. I'm in the middle of a conversation."

"Look here, dick for brains," I said, squaring my shoulders. "Think it's possible to move your ego ten steps over? I need a book. You know what those are, right? The things with words and pages?"

Adam's eyes narrowed. "Wow. Sure there isn't a pair of balls on you?"

"Sure there's a pair of balls on *you*?"

The other guy stepped between us and looked from me to Adam before clearing his throat. "Well, this has been fun, but the bell's about to ring. In case you forgot, Adam, tardies equal laps. Don't be the lap guy. We need you on the field."

"You ran laps yesterday, Tate," Adam answered. "Besides, the water girl needs a lesson in social status." He raised both hands so they were level, then slowly shifted them so one was higher. "This is me," he said, wiggling the hand closer to his face. "This is you." He wiggled the other one and grinned. "See the difference between us?"

"Yeah, you're the asshole," I answered.

Tate snorted, and Adam slugged him in the arm. Tate laughed louder.

"Fine," Adam said, stepping away. "Be friends with the water girl. I'm the smarter, more charming one, but it's your choice."

"I'm not the water girl!" I replied.

"Sure you're not." Adam winked and turned his back on me. Tate followed close behind.

Whatever. Adam could think what he wanted. I pulled my

book from my locker and hurried to English. When I got there, Mrs. Lories was already talking to the class. She paused midsentence, and everyone stared as I ducked my head and found a seat. Great. Now I was the tardy fish in the fishbowl.

The first empty desk I found was beside a girl with long blond hair. She wore a Pader High cheer hoodie and dark blue skinny jeans, and I'd seen her before. She was the girl I'd watched in the cafeteria. She might be the nicest person on earth, but she was too relatable to be around. Tomorrow I'd find a different desk.

I slid into the seat and placed my book in front of me.

"Claire," she whispered as I grabbed a pencil from my bag. "Claaaaaire."

I straightened and kept my eyes on the board. I didn't know her, and I didn't want to get in trouble when I'd already made a bad impression.

"Claire," she whispered again. When I still didn't answer, she paused and sat back in her chair. Her pencil rose to her lips, and she gnawed on the end. "Is her name Claire?" she murmured to herself. "I thought it was Claire, but what if her name was Mare or Cher? Crap. Never mind." She leaned forward, smiling as she tapped her pencil against the edge of my desk. I looked at her, and her smile widened. "Hi," she said. "We're on page five."

"Thanks," I answered.

I flipped to page five, and she relaxed, her blue eyes burning holes in my profile. When the bell rang, she was the first to stand.

"I'm Riley," she offered, slinging the strap of her messenger bag over her shoulder. "Pader High cheer captain and Luke Bryan fangirl."

"Claire," I replied. I grabbed my backpack and followed the rest of the students into the hall. Riley kept pace.

"I thought I recognized you," she said. "You're Case's sister, right? You two look the same—same nose, same hair color, same pale complexion."

I glanced at my bare arms. I was porcelain, not pale. There was a difference. "I'm not his sister," I answered. "He's my brother. On bad days, he's a stranger who shares my house."

She arched an eyebrow but paused to talk to a group of girls who passed us. One mentioned something cheer related, and Riley answered before catching up with me. "So," she continued. "Case is your brother? That's cool."

"Yep." I stopped and tried to find my way to Senior Hall. Riley kept talking.

"You moved into the Wilsons' old house, right? The one on Cheshire Lane?" I nodded, and she squealed. "Totally thought that was you! I'm two houses down. We should hang out sometime!"

We entered Senior Hall and Adam's friend Tate met us as we passed the first set of lockers. He wrapped an arm around Riley's shoulders, kissed her cheek, then glanced at me. "I don't think we've formally met," he said, extending a hand. "Tate Mack. Nice to meet you."

"Claire Collins. Nice to meet you, too."

Tate's brow furrowed as he whispered something to Riley.

"Yes," she answered, her voice loud. "This is Coach Collins's daughter. Case is her brother."

"I whispered it for a reason," Tate said, his eyes wide.

"Oops," she answered, shrugging.

Tate looked at me, his cheeks pinker than before. "Guess I'll go ahead and say sorry about Adam," he said, scratching his pointed jaw. "We didn't know who you were."

"And who am I?" I asked.

"The coach's daughter," Tate answered, grimacing. "As soon as Adam finds out your last name, he'll track you down and apologize. Don't want drama interfering with football, you know?"

I shifted my backpack and shook my head. "Actually, no. Apologies are apologies. If it isn't sincere, what's the point?"

"Um, good question." Tate cleared his throat and took a step in the opposite direction. He looked at Riley, cringing. "I'm going to class now," he said. "Riley, catch you later?"

"Bye, Tate," she answered.

Tate hurried away, and I stopped in front of my locker. Riley stayed at my side, scrolling through her phone while I traded out my books. When I was done, she crammed the phone in her pocket and smiled.

"I'm in computer science," she commented, motioning down the hall. "We should hang out, though. The rest of the people in our neighborhood are old. It'll be nice having someone my age within walking distance."

"Sounds great."

"Yay! See you later."

She pivoted, and I walked to government, eyeing my watch along the way. The ITV Lab, the largest classroom in the school, was luckily not too far from my locker. It was set up like a theater, with rectangular tables stretching from the middle of the room to staircases on either side. A massive flat-screen television covered the room's front wall, with individual speakers placed in every corner.

The room was colder than my other classrooms, and my short-sleeved T-shirt did nothing to ward off the chill. I rubbed my bare arms and found a table near the middle of the room. After unloading my textbook, notebook, and a pencil, I went back to rubbing my arms and checked my cell phone for a text from Seth. Nothing. My pulse raced and my frozen cheeks heated with embarrassment.

Why had I texted him? Now I was the clingy ex.

"Hello, sweetheart."

Adam's voice drew my attention to the bottom of the stairs. He was smiling, his eyes focused on me, and I groaned. This wasn't happening. Why was this happening?

"Miss me?" he asked.

"Not even a little."

He passed my table and knocked the book off my desk. A *bam* echoed around the room, making the entire class jump and look my way. I ducked my head, but Adam pointed at me.

"Blame the new girl," he said. "Had to find attention somehow."

He tried to continue up the stairs, but I stretched my foot out and sent him flailing into the table behind me.

"I'm not the only one seeking attention," I replied.

Adam straightened, his jaw set and his eyes narrowed. "Are you sure you want to mess with me?" he hissed, towering over me like I'd be intimidated. "Because I don't care if your dad is the coach. This ends one way: You'll lose."

"I never lose," I answered.

"That was before you met me." He plopped into a chair at the table behind me, his face tight as he leaned against the edge. "Don't say I didn't warn you, Collins."

"Don't say I didn't warn *you*."

Whether Adam believed me or not, I'd been in enough schools and dealt with enough people to handle myself. He was messing with the wrong girl. If he wasn't careful, he'd learn his lesson the hard way.

3

Four-Wheeling

"Okay, Claire. Which one is blue?"

Case stood in the hall, two blue button-downs in his hands. They were a shade apart, but they were both blue.

"You're good either way," I answered, returning my attention to unpacking. "Why?"

"Because Riley Cross is hot, and I'm trying to score a date." He frowned at the shirts, then combined the hangers in one hand. "I need to make sure my outfit is on point. Figured one of these shirts would do the trick."

I laughed at him. Case had as much chance with Riley as I had with a prince. It wasn't going to happen, regardless of his wardrobe.

"What's so funny?" he asked, entering my room. "I saw her watching me mow the other day. She wants my bod."

"Right, because a riding lawn mower screams sex appeal." I

shook my head and placed a pair of books on my computer desk. "You should try someone else," I urged. "She's with Tate. Might be a while before you get a shot."

"I give it to the end of the semester," Case answered. "She wants to let go but is too afraid to try something new."

"You're delusional."

"Yeah? Well, you're a dream crusher."

My phone beeped, and I crossed the fluffy teal rug in the center of the room. On my nightstand, the phone glowed. I frowned at the reminder about our monthly data usage. Almost two weeks and still nothing from Seth. My emotions were shot. I never should've sent the text.

"Is it Riley?" Case asked.

"Nope." I tossed the phone on my comforter and went back to my box.

He watched me, quiet as he fidgeted with the twinkling white lights I had strung across the top of my dresser. He was only this quiet when he wanted something. "So," he started, his tone too neutral to be good, "Mom told me you wanted to borrow the car. Baker Heights?"

"Is that a real question?" I pulled out a pair of picture frames and caught his judgmental stare. "What? You know how I feel. It's not like I've bottled it up."

"I get it, but I thought you were making friends."

"Riley can't replace my old friends," I said. "I had a life there, one Mom and Dad ripped away without considering how it would affect me. Nothing makes that okay." I placed the pictures facedown on my desk. They clanked together, scratching memories of people I'd left behind.

"Claire, I know you want to see him, but I really think—"

"Don't," I interrupted. "I know you're trying to pull the protective little brother card, but I made a deal with Mom and Dad. I'm visiting Baker Heights as soon as I can. If I'm there and I see Seth, I'll handle it the way *I* want to handle it."

"Fine," he answered, sounding like it was anything but fine. "I think you're making a mistake, but you do whatever you want."

His footsteps echoed down the hall. I closed the bedroom door behind him. All I wanted was one more year at Baker Heights. Case didn't understand. No one did. I lay across my bed, lost in thought.

"Claire!" my mom hollered.

I swiped the back of my hand across my cheeks and cleared my throat. "I'm sleeping!" I replied. My voice left me in a croak, so I cleared my throat again.

"Claire, company!" she said.

"Who?"

Silence.

"Who?" I repeated.

"Claire, company!" she yelled again.

I groaned and dragged myself from the mattress. My reflection stared at me from the large mirror on the far side of my room. My eyes were red and puffy, complemented by tear-stained cheeks. My hair was a mess of brown waves, tangled from being thrown into a ponytail, and my shirt was riddled with paint stains and dust. The shorts I'd stolen from Case were baggy around my waist, doing nothing to improve my appearance. I was a hot mess and in no shape for company.

"Claire!"

"Coming!" I yelled, hauling myself across the room.

Concealer sat inside a small makeup bag on my vanity. I slapped enough under my eyes to cover the puffiness, ran a brush through my hair, and inhaled. When I opened my door, Case sprinted by. He wore one of the blue button-downs and was frantically fastening the buttons.

"She's here," he whisper-yelled.

"Who's here?"

"Riley." His bedroom door slammed behind him.

I took the stairs to the bottom, hearing Riley's laugh as I reached the landing. She stood in the foyer with my mom, dressed in shorts, a plaid shirt with sleeves rolled to her elbows, and a pair of brown gladiator sandals. Her blond hair was curled in loose waves that were swept to one shoulder.

"Hey!" she said. "Sorry to barge in. I was in the neighborhood."

"You're two houses down," I answered. "You're always in the neighborhood."

"True." She pointed at the folded shirts in my mom's hands. "I was delivering this year's spirit shirts, and your house was the last stop. Since it's Saturday and I'm free the rest of the day, I thought you might want to hang out. We can do whatever, as long as it isn't English."

"Thanks," I started, "but I'm not feeling too well. Maybe a different—"

"Nonsense," my mom cut in.

I gawked at her, but she smiled at me with a shameless look of encouragement.

"Go hang out with your friend," she said. "Unpacking can wait. Those boxes will still be here when you get back."

I sucked in a breath and shook my head. My mind was on

Seth, and I didn't want to be a pessimistic stick-in-the-mud. Any other day? Okay. Today I couldn't do it. "I'll even let you two borrow the car," my mom said. "Case is here for the day, so it's not like he'll need it." I shot her a look that read *stop it*, but she ignored me and moved to the hall. "I'll get you girls the keys. Be right back."

"Awesome! Thanks, Mrs. Collins." Riley looked at me, excited. "Meet you outside in ten?"

"Sure," I answered, not even bothering to sound chipper.

Riley disappeared outside, letting in the afternoon heat through the doorway. My mom returned a few seconds later, almost colliding with Case as he jumped off the bottom of the stairs.

"Point me in her direction," Case said, smoothing his hair.

"You're too late." I snatched the keys from my mom and stalked up the stairs to change.

"Where did she go?!" my mom asked, turning to me.

"She's outside," I griped. "And congratulations on meddling mother of the year. You can expect your certificate by the end of the week."

She frowned, her hands finding her hips. "Claire."

"Bye, Mom."

* * *

"We're here!" Riley said, closing the car door. "Sorry, we stopped and grabbed Sonic."

The smell of livestock carried on the breeze slanting the overgrown blades of grass around us. The grass scratched my bare ankles as I followed Riley across the yard. Tate stood in front of a crimson-colored barn, with white trim along the doors and a metal roof that gleamed beneath the sweltering sun. He crossed his arms as Riley stopped in front of him.

"I brought Claire," she pointed out. "Hope that's okay."

His brown eyes settled on me, and he shrugged. "I'm cool with it, but I'm not the only one that matters."

"Adam can get over it," Riley answered. "If he doesn't, he can leave."

"Adam?" I repeated.

"The one and only," Riley said, motioning at a black Chevy as it rolled through the steel gates at the front of the property. Four-door and streaked with dirt, the truck pulled up to the barn with music so loud it shook the truck from the inside out.

"Speaking of which," Riley said. "I need to talk to him. He was supposed to let me know which players are helping with Friday's pep rally and he didn't."

"He's busy."

"So am I." She waited until Adam's dark tennis shoes hit the grass, then asked, "Hey, who's giving the pep talk at Friday's pep rally?"

"Hey to you, too."

He closed the door and crammed the keys in his pocket. He wore black athletic shorts, a gray Pader High practice shirt, and a matching black cap tugged so low it hit the brim of his sunglasses. His jaw clenched as his face tilted my direction.

"Thought it was the three of us," he said, returning his attention to Riley. "What changed?"

"I was tired of being the only girl," she answered.

He frowned. "Tate, you okay with this?"

"I don't care either way," Tate said. He grabbed one of the barn's doors and tried to tug it open. When it didn't budge, he looked at Adam, who hadn't moved an inch. "Going to stand there and watch me do this, or you feel like making yourself useful?"

"That depends," Adam snapped. "Are you going to pretend like you forgot to mention her being here?"

Tate straightened. "I didn't know she was coming. Now, quit being an ass and help me with the damn door."

I felt like the awkward duck who intruded on a planned event. "I can head out," I said, turning toward the car. "I need to finish unpacking. Riley, can you catch a ride home with Tate?"

"No."

Adam joined Tate at the door, still looking pissed. "It's fine," he grumbled. "If you leave, Riley will nag us the rest of the afternoon. Not dealing with it."

"It's true," Riley agreed. "You leave, and he'll wish you would've stayed."

The barn doors slid open, and the boys stepped inside. The smell of hay filled the dry air, but I didn't see any. There was nothing but a vacant concrete floor, lit by sunlight that streamed through the doors.

"This is where we hold parties," Riley said, spinning a circle in the middle of the room.

"Victory parties," Tate added.

He pulled the handle on a door at the back, and it opened onto a storage room with four-wheelers inside. They were lined up in three rows of three. Tate grabbed the keys before pointing at the corresponding vehicles.

"Helmets are one size fits all," he said. "Don't get on a four-wheeler without one."

"Afraid I'll damage my pretty face?" Adam teased.

"Afraid I'll damage the coach's daughter," Tate replied. He winked at me and found the last four-wheeler in my line.

Adam pulled the shades from his eyes. He stared at me, skeptical. "Doubt she can even work one," he said. "Collins, need a diagram and step-by-step directions on how to make it go?"

I flipped him off before I realized what I'd done.

"Someone needs to learn manners!" he said, laughing.

"Someone needs to learn to be nice," I answered.

"Probably." He traded his hat for a helmet and steered the vehicle toward the door. Riley followed close behind.

Tate looked at me as I mounted the four-wheeler. My hands ran across uneven rubber handles, trying to decide which of two handles was the clutch. "You can ride with Riley," he offered, tugging a helmet over his curly hair.

"I've got it." I chose a lever, and the four-wheeler thrust forward. "See. No biggie."

"Suit yourself."

The four-wheeler hummed to life, the sound of the engine resonating off the barn's metal walls as I drove toward the front. Riley sat outside the doors, idling as she snapped selfies. She crammed her phone in her back pocket, then pointed at an overgrown field of grass.

A rusted gate, closed with a thick piece of chain, sat between us and the pasture. Adam had rehitched it from the inside. He was already back on his four-wheeler, jumping over mounds in the distance. Tate sped past us and unhitched the gate. Once we were through, he secured the chain and joined Adam.

Riley stared at me behind her helmet. "Think we can speed this up?" she asked. "I can stay with you, but at this rate I'll be ninety before we make it to the jumps."

I nodded, and she raced away, throwing up bits of grass as she crossed the field. I was stuck on turtle pace, with no idea how to change the speed. I messed with the clutch, sending the four-wheeler forward in a lurch.

"Hey!" I heard Adam yell.

I turned and spotted Adam's four-wheeler racing toward me. When he got within a few feet, he turned his vehicle sharp, spraying mud over my helmet, shirt, shorts, and bare legs. I sat on the leather seat, drenched, as I stared at him.

"Geez, Claire. What happened to you?" he asked, coming to a stop. His whole body shook with laughter, making me want to strangle him. "Oh, wait. I know. Me."

My hands curled around my knees, and my fingernails dug into my skin. He had to be kidding me! "Why did you throw mud on me?! This was a cute outfit!"

"It's horse water," Adam clarified, pulling his helmet off and resting it on his lap. He pointed at the large metal trough to our right. My stomach rolled as I took in the frothy puddle around it. "It's not my fault you were sitting in the spray zone," he continued. "I needed to turn, and there you were. Oops."

"Is that what's on me?" I asked, bile rising in my throat as a bubble popped in the mud. "Tell me you're joking. You are joking, right?"

"Nope."

I pulled my helmet off and threw it at him. "You're such an asshole, Adam! That's full of bacteria and—"

"You're covered in it?"

"Yes!" I stared at my dirty legs and cringed. "I can't handle this. I'm going to vomit."

"Are you serious?"

I gagged and held up a hand to halt him.

He crammed his helmet on his head and motioned toward the gate. "Ew. Do it out there. I don't want to drive through your nastiness."

I inhaled and slowly released my breath. "I'll get you back," I said. "This will bite you in the butt, and you'll be begging for my forgiveness."

"Really, sweetheart? I'd love to see you try."

He sped off, and I gagged again. I didn't know much about Pader, but I was positive about one thing. Adam Meade was a pest. Eventually, I'd squash him.

Revenge

"Plans for Friday?"

I glanced at Riley and crammed two oversized books in my locker. "School," I answered. "More specifically, a test in English and a study guide for government."

"Oh! Right. About that English test . . ."

I knew what she was getting at. "We can study at my house," I volunteered. "Let me know when you want to meet. I'll order pizza."

"Have I said you're the best?"

I nodded and glanced around her, catching sight of Adam as he approached his locker. He had a girl with him, poor thing. He leaned against the metal with his arms crossed, smiling at her as she talked. If he wasn't such a dick, he would've been attractive. His good looks faded the moment he splattered horse water all over me.

I tossed my backpack over my shoulder and shut the locker. Adam glanced at Riley and me as we passed.

"Headed to study hall?" Riley asked, turning so she walked backward. Her eyes were on Adam as she pointed at the girl, then shook her head. "Wish I had study hall," she continued. "Sounds fun."

"Get the rest of your class credits this semester. They might switch your schedule after Christmas." She was still walking backward, so I turned and walked backward, too. "Is this a new thing?" I asked. "Did I somehow miss out on a trend?"

"No," Riley answered, frowning. "Just trying to keep Adam from going for the wrong girl yet again. Dude thinks with the wrong head, and he doesn't get how his actions affect me. Every time he breaks a heart, the girl wants to hang out with me to get him back. I can't do it anymore. I'm tired of avoiding half the school's female population. That includes some pretty pissed-off cheerleaders I have to be on a team with."

"Tell him to keep it in his pants." I turned toward the library. "Or set him up with someone he likes. There has to be someone."

"Adam doesn't like anyone. That's the problem."

I shrugged. "Can't change people who don't want to be changed."

"But what if they want to be changed and don't know how?"

"Deep thoughts by Riley Cross," I said. "Will think about it and get back to you."

"Please do," she answered, splitting off toward another hall.

The smell of aged books and lemon-scented wood polish hit me as I stepped through the library doors. Mrs. Jenkins, the librarian, stood behind her desk, fiddling with computer keys.

I took a seat at one of the tables and tossed my backpack on the ground. Adam jogged by a few seconds later, followed by the bell. He was late to ag class, but my dad's running punishment would pale in comparison to my special treat.

"Mrs. Jenkins," I said, moping toward her desk. "I think I forgot my government book in the bathroom. Can I go check? If someone takes it, I don't want to have to buy the school a replacement."

"Sure, but try not to dally."

"Yes, ma'am."

I grabbed my backpack and hurried through the door, stepping into the breezeway, where the aroma of greasy cafeteria food made my stomach grumble. The hall was clear, and the only noise was the clanking of spoons from the lunchroom ladies.

My time was limited, so I scuttled down the hall and quietly found the back doors. With one swift movement, I was outside and running down the sidewalk.

Humidity clung to my arms as I weaved between rows of cars. Adam's Chevy sat in the third row. It gleamed like a ray of sunshine, freshly washed and waxed. I glanced around for any lingering students. The coast was clear. I took a breath to steady my rapid pulse, then curled my fingers around the tailgate and hoisted myself up.

With my body flush against the bed, I unzipped my bag and retrieved two tubes of shoe polish. The black one, the larger of the two, smelled like chemicals. I scrunched my nose and slunk forward, raising my hand to smear the polish against the glass. Top to bottom, side to side, the window was blacked out. Nothing could be seen in or out.

Sweat coated my neck as I hurdled the tailgate and landed on the gravel. I took another look around the parking lot, then blacked out the windows on the driver's side. Like a ninja, I moved to the passenger side and repeated the process.

When everything, including the side mirrors, was coated in black, I slid around the trunk and scrawled #winning in white polish against Adam's driver's side door. My breath left me in short spurts as I ran to my car, dropped the evidence in my trunk, and hurried back into the school.

I was still hyped on adrenaline when I found Riley in the cafeteria the period after. I sat across from her and Tate, studying my chicken strips as the pair talked with the rest of the table. Adam was gone. I didn't know if that was a good thing or a bad one.

"We need to talk about Thursday's pregame plans," Riley said. "We doing the usual? Burgers at Big Sal's, then the game?"

"I'm down," Tate agreed. "Claire, you in?"

"That's nice of you," I started. "But I—" A cafeteria door slammed open, and Adam stormed across the tile, his cheeks red and his jaw clenched. Oh crap.

"But you what?" Riley said.

"D-don't eat meat."

Adam found our table, green eyes blazing as he dropped into the chair across from me. The intensity behind his glare made me wriggle. If looks could kill, I'd be dead on the floor.

"What are you talking about?" he muttered through clenched teeth.

"Big Sal's," Riley answered. She bit into her pizza and shrugged. "I was asking Claire if she wanted to go with us on Thursday, but she doesn't eat meat. Kudos to you, by the way. Tried to go vegetarian a while back, but only lasted a week. Chicken did me in."

"Funny," Adam stated, pointing at my food. "Claire's eating chicken right now. Care to explain?"

Confused, I looked at Riley. "I'm a vegetarian?"

"Seems like it," Adam answered. "Which means you won't mind if I have a few of these." He slid my tray across the table, offering Tate a couple of chicken strips while he finished off the rest. "Question," he said, swallowing as he stared at me. "Someone messed with my truck."

"That isn't a question. Usually, questions have a question in them. Try something with who, why, or what."

He chuckled, his senior ring catching the light as he scratched his jaw. "Okay," he said. "What happened to my truck?"

"Oh, that? Not sure. Heard it was a girl you pissed off, but I didn't catch her name. I'm sure there's plenty of options."

"You think you're funny," he hissed, "but I take a class with you. I recognize your handwriting."

"No proof," I said, smiling.

"I don't need proof." He leaned over the table and arched a brow. "I do find it funny, though. You can't get my attention another way, so you have to resort to stupid little games like screwing with my truck. It's pathetic, Collins."

"Pathetic?" I repeated, my heart pounding out of my chest. "Hate to break it to you, but you're nothing special. You're a mediocre quarterback with his head shoved so far up his ass it's a wonder you can see a football at all. There's tons of guys like you, Meade. I've seen better. I've *dated* better."

The table grew silent, and the rest of the room followed.

"That sounds like the bitter ramblings of a lonely, unwanted girl," Adam stated, his voice a whisper. "Have you always been like this, or is it because I hurt your feelings? Is it because you're stuck in Pader and you hate it? Is it because my friends are the only ones who have gone out of their way to be nice to you? Or, more likely, is it because everyone likes your brother, but they don't like you?"

My blood heated as I sat there, slack jawed at the harshness in his words. He'd picked me apart in front of the entire senior class. By the smugness on his face, he didn't even care.

The sound of my chair sliding against the tile was deafening.

"Claire—"

I ignored Riley and stormed out of the cafeteria. My walls were cracked, and I needed to get out of the storm before Hurricane Adam rolled through and shattered my windows.

I spent the rest of the lunch period in my car. Riley was waiting for me when I got to English. She sat at her desk, her chin in her hands, as I moved through the aisle and found my seat beside her.

Adam crossed a line. No amount of talking to Riley would remedy what he broke.

When the bell rang for dismissal, I grabbed my backpack and exited the room. The trek down Senior Hall was made in record speed, and I ducked into government without stopping to drop my English books at my locker. I was first in class, so I sifted through social media while the rest of the students filed through the door. That was a mistake.

Tonight was Senior Welcome Night at Baker Heights—one of the most talked-about events of the year. The bonfire, held on the outskirts of town, was put on by Student Council and the Booster Club. All my old friends would be there; Seth would be there; and it would be plastered all over Facebook, Instagram, and Twitter like a flashing neon sign for everything I was missing.

My heart ached for company; my soul sought comfort; and I was hours away with no possibility of getting there. It was like knowing Ed Sheeran would be in town, but the tickets were sold out. I'd see the pictures everywhere, unable to rein in my jealousy. I couldn't handle it, and the event hadn't even happened.

Adam entered with the bell. I heard his voice as he ascended the steps, but I couldn't look at him. He dropped a folded piece of notebook paper beside my book. My name was scrawled across the top in slanted letters. I avoided it like the plague. Who knew what horrible things he'd put inside?

When the bell rang, I stood. Adam's exaggerated sigh came from behind me as he hoisted his backpack over his shoulder, closed the distance, and stopped beside my table. His jaw was tight as he pulled the paper from the desk, unfolded it, and pointed at the words.

"I'm sorry," he read, lifting his gaze. "I didn't mean to take it that far."

"Thanks," I answered, busying myself with my backpack. It was an apology, but a forced one.

"So, we're good?" he asked.

"What do you think?" I slid the backpack over my shoulder and pushed in my chair. Adam blocked my path. "Can I go now?" I continued with a frown. "I've got another class. I can't get there if you don't move."

"We didn't get off on the best foot," he answered.

"No, we didn't," I agreed. "The first time you met me, you ordered me to bring you ice. The last time I checked, that isn't the best way to introduce yourself."

"I didn't order you," he defended. "I asked in my own special way."

"You ordered."

He moved and descended the stairs behind me. "It was a small request, on a hot day, and I was already tired," he explained. "Sorry if I didn't add a 'please' to the end."

"'Please' would've made you less of a jerk. Next time, add it."

His left cheek dimpled. "Noted."

He followed me into the hall, thick crowds of students parting for him like they'd burn at his touch. When I found my locker a minute later, he was still by my side.

"If you think stalking is a good way to apologize, you're wrong." I hung my backpack on the hook and unzipped it. "It's creepy and desperate."

"Oh?" He took a step back, his hands outstretched in front of him. "Well, I guess I'll take my creepy and desperate self over there."

"You and yourself have fun."

"Trust me, we will."

He winked and sauntered across the tile, girls watching him as he walked. Why were the hot ones always evil? It was like the universe needed their personality to be ugly so it balanced out their handsome exterior.

I was still stewing on that question when I got home. Thankfully, the gorgeous bachelor on TV disproved my theory. He was one part adventurous, one part emotional, one part honest, and one part rugged stud. It was a vast improvement from what Pader High had to offer.

Nestled on the couch in my pajamas, I crammed a handful of popcorn in my mouth and swooned. Movement on the porch drew my attention. Case pushed his way in, interrupting the rose ceremony halfway through one girl's meltdown.

"Wow, sis, you look hideous."

"Wow, Case, you smell like ass." My nose crinkled, and I stared at the television. "They make these things called showers. I'm sure there's a few in the field house. You should use them."

"Fine, no present for you," he answered, rounding the couch with a Sonic cup in his hand.

I smiled and greedily outstretched my hand. "You don't even know how bad I need a limeade. Thanks, Case."

He took a sip, dashing my hopes and dreams. "My limeade, not yours. The present is your math binder. You left it in Dad's office. Adam said you had homework, so I grabbed it on our way out."

"Adam is the root of all evil."

"Most girls think I'm the opposite. Nice to have a fresh point of view," Adam said as he walked through the front door, hauling a box. He dropped it on the wood and brushed his hands against dark jeans. "By the way, there's an overly aggressive squirrel on your front porch. I thought those things were day creatures, but this one tried to claw my face off!"

"Meeko is a good judge of character," I replied.

"Claire named the squirrel," Case added, looking at Adam. "It's a weird thing she does. Just go with it."

"Okay," Adam answered, drawing out the word. "Name the tree, too?"

I pulled a blanket from the back of the couch and tugged it over my head. If I pretended not to exist, maybe he'd leave me alone. The blanket was immediately tugged off, replaced with Adam's face. So much for my peaceful night with the nation's most tantalizing bachelor.

"Is there something you need?" I asked. "I assume you gave Case a ride home. Thanks. He's home now. You can leave."

"Adam's staying for dinner," Case said.

My face paled as I stared at my brother. "Adam's not staying for dinner," I replied. "Adam has a perfectly delicious dinner waiting at his own house. Don't you, Adam?"

"My grandma's out tonight. My schedule is wide open."

My eyes narrowed. If this was their idea of a prank, their sense of humor sucked.

"Really, why are you here?" I asked, staring at him.

"Dinner," he replied. "Ran into your mom outside the field house. She was carrying a box—"

"Window decals for the team," Case interjected.

"—and I helped her," Adam said. "In return, your dad invited me to dinner. Wanted to talk about football scholarships, anyway. He has scouts calling. Who was I to turn him down?"

I groaned and stood, pulling the blanket around my shoulders as I marched toward the stairs. My dad and I would be having an enlightening conversation after the meal. He needed to know the boundaries between football and Claire's personal space.

"Also," Adam added as I reached the stairs, "your dad mentioned steaks on the menu. Wasn't aware you ate steak."

"It's her favorite," Case commented, stealing a handful of my popcorn. "Every time Dad grills, Claire is first in line. She'll finish off two, easy."

Adam cocked his head to the side and my cheeks heated. "Really? That's interesting," he answered. "Tell me, are you a rare, medium-well, or well-done kind of girl?"

I scowled at Adam over the rail. "I hate you."

"Get in line."

* * *

As fate would have it, not only was Adam a huge suck-up when he needed to be, but he was also a great liar. Mom was tonight's griller. He ate my mom's steak without gagging once. That was a feat by all standards, given that my mom charbroiled all steaks until they were almost inedible.

"Dinner was delicious, Mrs. Collins."

Adam stood and pushed in his chair while my mom watched with an adoring look she never gave me.

I mimicked the movement and followed him to our kitchen. My dad stood inside, leaning against the marble counter while gnawing on a burnt crescent roll.

"Heard from the scouts today," he said, addressing Adam as we put our plates in the sink. "They're coming to the game on Friday, and they want to see how you run the ball. We'll discuss it more tomorrow, but I wanted to keep you in the loop."

"Awesome. Thanks, Coach." Adam's gaze flitted to me, and he withdrew his keys from his pocket. He looked hesitant, but he cleared his throat and wiped the emotion from his face. "I need to get going. Thank you for the meal. I appreciate it."

"You're welcome anytime," my dad answered.

He grabbed a dish from my mom as she entered behind us.

I took that as the prime moment to nudge Adam away from them. It was no easy feat considering his size and ability to withstand the force of my biceps. Thankfully, though, he gave up resisting and let me push him out the door.

"Okay!" I said. "Have a good night."

"Walk me to the truck."

"Um, no."

I moved to shut the door, but he caught it. "Walk me to the truck," he repeated.

"Why? Want to berate me more?"

"I already apologized," he answered, heading down the sidewalk. His truck windows were clear of polish, and the driver's side gleamed once more. "Besides, you screwed up my stuff. I was allowed to be pissed."

"Being pissed and crossing a line are two different things," I said, trailing behind him.

Once we reached his truck, he turned and leaned his back against it. "Again, already apologized for what I said. Can't do much more than that."

"You could be nicer in general."

"I'm not a nice guy. Think that's a little out of the question." Adam opened the door and slid inside. He cranked the truck, and the dull hum of classic rock played from the speakers, breaking through the quiet night. "Tell your parents thanks again for the dinner," he said. "It was great. I had fun."

"We both know family dinners aren't fun," I replied.

"Or maybe you don't appreciate them," he returned.

The comment struck me as he closed the door and pulled away from the curb. His taillights disappeared down another road, leaving me beneath the streetlight with nothing but dread settling in the pit of my stomach.

Adam was the epitome of annoying and the poster child for arrogant football player, but I seemed to be the only one who felt that way. Either I was missing something, or the problem lay with me.

Tales of Tofu

"She likes me. You can tell me she doesn't, but my heart speaks the truth."

"You're delusional."

Case glanced at a pair of girls as they passed. I slugged him on the shoulder to regain his attention.

"You're delusional *and* hormonal," I corrected.

"Don't judge me. I'm the one with the cash." He pulled a wallet from his back pocket and retrieved a pair of ten-dollar bills. "Before I give these to you," he said, raising the money out of reach, "please tell me why you deserve an extra allowance when I'm the one who bought gas."

"I get an extra allowance because I put up with you," I replied. "My payment should be way more than twenty bucks."

"You need to work on being more persuasive," he answered. I attempted to grab the money, but Case shook his head. "I'll give this to you, but I get the car next weekend," he said. "No car. No money."

"I can't promise you the car. Mom and Dad haven't told me when I can visit Baker Heights. I won't make a deal I can't keep."

"It won't be next weekend," he answered. "The game is in town, and you're supposed to be there. Remember?"

"Not participating in football activities. Shouldn't matter either way." I tried for the money again, but Case kept it out of reach. "Please give me the money," I pleaded. "I'm asking you as nicely as possible."

"Mow the lawn Saturday and you can have it."

"I'm not bartering for money Mom and Dad already said I could have!"

"Then the money stays with me." He crammed the tens in his pocket and shrugged.

I started to protest but caught myself. Maybe Case was onto something.

"Claire!" Riley's ribbon-wrapped ponytail bounced as she passed computer science and stopped beside Case. "You riding with me to Big Sal's? We can leave as soon as the pep rally is prepped for tomorrow."

"I would," I answered, "but I forgot my money at home."

Case pulled the tens from his pocket and handed them over. "No problem. I have some money you can borrow." He winked at Riley and pushed a hand through his dark hair. "What time will you be there? I might join."

"You're not invited," I replied.

Case gawked at me as I moved toward government. The answer was rude, but the last thing I needed was him hitting on Riley in front of Tate. He wouldn't live to see October.

I reached the government room right before the bell rang. Adam was already in his seat. He leaned across the table as I slid onto my chair.

"Look who decided to join us," he said.

"It was a hard choice, but I figured someone had to put up with you."

"Hey, your parents love me," he answered.

I pulled my notebook from my backpack and turned in my seat. "What do you want? A billboard with your name on it?"

"A billboard would be cool," he said, nodding, "but I'd prefer a personalized sign for tomorrow night's game. I'm thinking block lettering and a little bit of glitter, with 'Adam's number one fan' written on it. I'll even sign it, if you want."

"You're something else. You know that?"

"Yep."

The class monitor dimmed the light. Our government class was part of a long-distance learning program, given through a junior college. The professor lectured through a TV screen, but we were expected to keep notes and finish the assignments like every other college student.

Adam stood the minute class was dismissed. "Tell me," he said, slinging his backpack over his shoulder. "You ordering vegetarian tonight, or is your inner carnivore screaming for succulent beef?" I ignored him and finished jotting notes. "Earth to Claire," he said. "C.C. phone home?"

"Do you come up with this material on your own, or do you pay someone to do it?" I shut my notebook and stood. "If you pay someone, ask for better material."

"Funny."

I went to my locker and twisted the combination lock. Adam

stopped beside me, his arms crossed as he surveyed the inside. "Need something?" I asked, switching my government book for computer science.

"Nope." He tilted his head for a better view, then poked an Auburn magnet stuck to the back of the door. "Tiger fan?"

"More than you know." I slammed the locker, just missing his fingers. "Got to go. Mr. Acua hates tardies."

"See you at Big Sal's?"

"Yes. I'll be the vegetarian in the corner booth."

* * *

"I feel like I'm coming down with something."

"Yeah, football fever."

I scowled at my mom. "That's the best you've got? Now I know where Case gets his humor."

"My humor is amazing," she said. "You're just mad I'm funnier than you."

"Whatever helps you sleep at night."

I leaned against the counter and glanced at the clock on the wall. My mom followed my gaze, tossed a pair of shears on the counter, and untied her apron.

"Why didn't you tell me what time it was?" she asked. "You're supposed to be there in five minutes." She crossed the polished wood floors, flipped the lock on the front door, then turned the OPEN sign to CLOSED. "Who's going to be there?" she asked, pivoting. "Anyone named Adam?"

"Ugh. You're too involved in my social life," I groaned.

"I'm involved because I care."

We entered the shop's back room, where multihued flowers

filled the shelves and their fragrance ran rampant. The iridescent lights flickered off, and my mom opened one of the large double doors. Warm afternoon air joined the already humid room.

"You're lucky I'm the kind of mom who gets involved," she continued. "I should have your undying gratitude."

"You do. It's hidden behind eternal embarrassment."

I followed her to the white SUV. Behind its tinted windows, the black leather interior radiated heat. I was careful not to leave my bare legs flush against the seat too long. I would wear red marks on the back of my thighs for hours.

Country music played on the radio, but it was drowned out by the air conditioner I cranked to max speed.

"So," my mom said as she backed out of the space, "seems like you and Riley are becoming quick friends. Happy to see you're giving Pader a try."

"That was the deal," I answered. I shifted and glanced at her across the middle console. "Speaking of our deal, any news on when I can go to Baker Heights?"

"Right now, it's looking like Thanksgiving," she said.

I sighed and slumped against the leather. Leave it to my mom to crush my hopes and dreams.

"That's forever," I grumbled.

"Sorry." The car hummed as she turned a corner and increased her speed. Vintage shops whizzed by in a blur of red brick, white signs, and cracked concrete. "I would let you go sooner," she continued, "but football season is the busiest time of the year."

"I don't care about football. Football got me into this mess."

"We've had this discussion," she answered, her tone turning flat. "Your dad couldn't turn down the offer. It was too good to—"

"Dad could've turned it down," I interrupted, "but he chose not to."

Her lips spread into a thin line, and I shifted my attention to my phone. Across the screen, a text from Seth appeared. My heart quickened, but my hopes fell at **Do you have my calculator?**

I moved a hand to my heart and willed away the ache settled there. The text was a far cry from the **I miss you** I sent him on the first day of school.

Thinking we'd get back together was ridiculous, but I held out hope. This was a punch to the gut. Seth didn't want me. He wanted his calculator. How tragic could this get?

No, I answered.

The SUV slowed. The school parking lot held only a small group of students and a handful of cars. Clad in red, black, and white, Riley stood in the middle. Her hands were on her hips as she spoke with the students.

"I know that wasn't the answer you wanted," my mom said, putting the car in park, "but you're the happiest you've been in a long time. You're smiling again. You're going out and doing things. I was so worried about you, and now that you're moving on, I'm worried what going back will do. It's selfish, but I don't want to lose you again, hun. I just want you to be happy."

My heart ached. I understood where she was coming from, but I could handle it. I could go back without letting Seth derail my happiness.

"I'll be fine," I answered. "I promise."

"Then I'll talk to your dad about moving up the trip."

"Thanks, Mom."

The sun was almost parallel with the school, but heat clung to the air as I got out of the car and shut the door. Riley met me and waved at my mom, who returned the gesture as she backed away from the gym.

"Ready for food?" Riley asked.

"Yep."

I followed her across the gravel and slid into a tiny red car a few spaces down. Within minutes, we pulled into an unmarked space at a small diner. A white Mustang sat beside us. On the back window, a football emblem read MACK.

"Tate beat us here," she said.

She pulled the key from the ignition and led the way through a set of glass doors. A small metal bell rang with our entrance, and the smell of french fries bid us hello.

"Welcome to Big Sal's!" a voice called.

On our right, positioned behind an off-white counter, a middle-aged man stood opposite Tate. He shifted his attention back to the notepad and continued to jot Tate's order while Riley closed the door behind us.

"Couldn't wait?" she teased.

"Nope," Tate replied. He pulled her in for a hug and motioned at me with his free hand. "New addition," he said, addressing the man. "That should score me a discount."

"If I gave you a discount, you'd eat this place out of business," the guy answered. He winked at Riley and looked at me again. "Name's Sal. Happy to have you here."

"Thanks."

"Best burgers this side of Charlotte," he said. "You'll be here once a week like these two. Where's Meade? He want a burger, too?"

"Probably," Riley replied, "but Claire can't eat meat. Got anything else?"

I cringed. I could tell Riley the truth and be the newest liar on campus, or I could suck it up and deal with the consequences. Which was worse, embarrassment or faking vegetarianism?

Before I could decide, Sal answered, "Got some tofu in the fridge." He scribbled down *tofu burger*. Once he had all the orders, he handed each of us a Styrofoam cup. "Machine's in the back," he instructed. "We do free refills, and if the guys win tomorrow, there'll be a fifty-percent discount on ice cream."

"We'll win," Tate assured. "Just make sure you've got plenty of the Butterfinger kind."

"Always do," Sal replied.

Riley pulled away from the pair and ushered me across the linoleum floor. We stopped in front of a large soda dispenser. The machine sat beneath framed sports memorabilia that extended the length of the wall. Football team photos ranged from present day to the early fifties. They were mixed with various cheerleading photos and three retired jerseys.

"This is my favorite place in town," she said. "I love all the pictures. My mom's in a few."

"I like it, too," I replied. "It's old-school, and these pictures are awesome."

After we filled our drinks, Riley moved to a booth in the far corner and slid across the red leather upholstery. "Finally got the pep rally stuff done," she said, setting her cup on the table. "You would've gotten recruited to help if I wasn't done when you got there."

I took a seat across from her and shrugged. "Wouldn't be the first time I prepped for a pep rally," I answered. "Last year it took hours to get everything set up. The cheer coach and the team captain could never agree where to put the signs."

"You were a cheerleader?" I nodded, and she shook her head. "Bummer you didn't move here sooner. We could've been on the team together."

"Been on what team?" Tate asked, taking a seat beside Riley.

"Claire was a cheerleader," she said. "If she would've gotten here in May, we could've been on the same team." Riley leaned against the table. "I feel like such a terrible friend for not knowing this. What else did you do before you moved here? Where did you move from? Were you in band? Did you play sports? Any boyfriends?"

"Boyfriends?" Adam slid into the booth beside me and wedged me against the wall. I scowled at his profile as he sipped from his cup. "Who has a boyfriend?" he continued, looking at Riley. "Besides you."

"Why do you care, Mr. I Don't Do Relationships?" she said.

"Inquiring minds."

She rolled her eyes, and Tate chuckled. "Riley's still upset about you standing up Brooke. She'll deal."

"It was the week before school started, and she's still angry," Riley said. "You deal with mood swings and passive-aggressive comments and see how happy it makes you." She scowled at Adam. "The next time you can't make a date, call the girl and let her know. Brooke sat here for over an hour waiting on you."

"I was busy," he answered, "and my phone was dead. Besides, I told you I wasn't interested in Brooke, and you set us up anyway. Next time, check before you volunteer me to go out with one of your friends."

"Sorry. I was trying to help you find something to focus on, other than football. Don't worry. I won't set you up with anyone else," Riley replied.

She glanced at me, but I looked at Sal, who reached the table with a large red tray. Thankfully, food eased Riley's and Adam's moods.

"Two number fives," Sal said, placing the baskets in front of Riley and Tate. "One number eight."

He sat a basket with two mouth-watering double cheeseburgers in front of me, and my mouth dropped. If this was what tofu looked like, I'd happily eat it every day of the week.

"I'll take that," Adam said, sliding the basket over as I moved in for the kill.

"But that's—"

Sal sat a basket in front of me and my throat knotted. The patty was a nice golden brown, but something didn't smell right. The sandwich smelled like nuts with fishy undertones.

"Everything good?" Sal asked. The rest of the group nodded. "Great! Let me know if you need any ketchup."

Sal backed away while I tilted my head toward Adam's cheeseburgers. When he cut into them, revealing cheese-covered, salty strips of pork, I wanted to cry. My nasty-smelling burger couldn't compare to cheesy bacon.

"I can't believe Sal had tofu burgers," Riley said. "I thought you'd be limited to fries. This is way better."

"Yay," I said, my voice flat.

I poked the burger with my fork, then looked at Riley's and Tate's food. This wasn't fair. The world hated me.

"Who wants fries when you have such a health-conscious meal?" Adam teased. Grease dripped from the bottom of his burger as he raised it and took a bite. He hummed with satisfaction and nodded at my food. "Better eat up," he said, swallowing. "Wouldn't want it to get cold."

"Yeah, Claire. Try it," Riley agreed.

My instincts told me to run, but my conscience told me to be polite. I sniffed the burger again and placed the bun to my lips. One bite and my taste buds were sacrificed to a bitter, nutty-tasting sponge. I gagged and willed the food down my throat, suffocated by the rancid smell of the burger and the accompanying flavor of mayo and . . . an itch spread down my neck.

No, no, no.

"Shit, Claire. What's wrong with your face?"

I ignored Adam and threw off the wheat bun. Beneath it, staring at me in its green glory, sat a bed of mayo-covered spinach.

"Are those hives?" Riley asked, standing as I pushed Adam out of the booth ahead of me.

I followed her concerned gaze to the splotches on my arms. Red hives extended from my wrists to my elbows, and burned every inch they covered. I tried not to scratch them as they spread beneath my tee. I needed cortisone cream and Benadryl stat.

I booked it out of Big Sal's and pulled my phone from my pocket.

"Are you dying?" Adam asked, matching my stride as I walked to Riley's car.

"I'm allergic to spinach," I said. My mom's phone went to voice mail. I hung up and tried my dad instead.

"Are you deathly allergic?" he asked. "If so, could I have a time frame for how long it'll take you to keel over?"

"Shut up, Adam." My dad's phone went to voice mail. "Grr!" I clenched the phone in my fist and stared at the sky. It was getting harder and harder not to scratch my boobs. "No one's answering," I groaned. "I need medicine, or it'll get worse."

Adam pulled his keys from his pocket as Riley and Tate pushed through the doors. They held three paper bags and came to a stop beside us.

"Here," Riley said, handing one to Adam. "Sure you've got her?"

"Yes," Adam answered. "I'll get her home, no problem."

I looked from him to Riley, then back. "Oh, no you don't," I said. "Point me in the direction of the nearest pharmacy, and I'll be fine."

"You'd rather walk than let me drive you?" Adam asked, his mouth tilting at the corner.

"Um, yes." I gave into the burning sensation on my arm and scratched it with my nails. "Just tell me how to get to the pharmacy. This town is tiny. It can't be far."

"You're not walking," Riley said.

"Well, you can't drive her," Adam replied.

"He's right," Tate agreed. "It's the first Junior Varsity game of the season, and you're the cheer captain. You have to introduce the cheer team."

I moved my fingernails to the space between my shoulder blades. I couldn't reach the spot but needed to relieve the itch that flamed across my skin. Adam's hand gently wrapped around my biceps and turned me around. I glared at him over my shoulder.

"You won't reach it," he insisted. "You don't want me to touch you? Fine. Just trying to help."

I tried again but couldn't relieve the burn. I was torn between pride and need.

"Okay," I answered. "Scratch it. Scratch it now."

His fingernails scraped the fabric, and I let out an embarrassing sigh of relief. My attention returned to my arm, where hives continued to sprout.

"I'll take her," Adam repeated. "Call me with the score, and let me know how they do."

"Sure thing."

Riley and Tate got into their cars, but I didn't tell either good-bye. I was too distracted by what set of hives to scratch next.

"Think you can make it to my truck without looking weird?" Adam asked, pulling his hand away.

"Think *you* can make it to your truck without looking weird?" I replied.

He rolled his eyes and crossed the parking lot to his black Chevy. After unlocking the doors, he tugged open the passenger one and motioned inside.

"Don't say I never did anything for you," he said as I slid onto the seat.

"There's a first time for everything, Meade."

Skeptical

My mortal enemy drove me home. I expected sarcastic criticisms and snarky comments, but all I got was awkwardness wrapped in the shell of a broody six-foot teenager. When Adam reached my house, I exited the vehicle and ended the impromptu bonding moment as abruptly as it came.

The next day, at lunch, Adam talked to Riley and Tate but left me out of the conversation. In government, he sat behind me, burning holes through my skull. He was a statue with a scowl etched into his stone, and his radio silence was deafening.

I decided to confront him after class. He left the minute the bell rang.

At Riley's locker, my bare arms rested against cool metal as she loaded her backpack. Adam stood across from us, putting things in his locker while a girl tried to carry on a conversation with him. Adam kept his head ducked and his eyes on his locker. The only time he acknowledged her was when he asked her to hold his letter jacket.

"Did you make him drive me home?" I asked Riley, shifting my attention. "Or was it something he volunteered to do?"

"He volunteered," she said. She pulled her own letter jacket from the top of her locker and slung it over her arm. "Why?"

"Because he's been weird all day. I don't know how to handle him."

I tugged my lip between my teeth and took another glance. The girl was looking at the football patches sewn beneath MEADE. He took the jacket and shut the locker with a bang.

"I can ask him why he's being weird to you," Riley said, "but it comes with a price."

"What's the price?"

"Food at the game."

I watched Adam and the girl as they talked, my plans to skip the football game quickly unraveling.

"Fine," I agreed.

"Great!" Riley adjusted the red-and-black ribbon tossed around her blond hair and blew out a breath. "Also, before I forget to ask, do you have plans tomorrow? We're taking Tate's boat to Lake Wylie. I want you to come with us."

I hesitated. In theory, it sounded awesome. In reality, there was a college admissions essay and a stack of scholarship applications screaming my name. Auburn wasn't cheap; no four-year university was possible without financial aid. If I wanted to go there, fun was the sacrifice.

"I have scholarship things to work on," I said.

"Bring them along and do them in the sun," she replied. "The guys want to fish, so we'll be on the water for a while. It'll be perfect."

"I'll think about it."

Tate approached and rested his arm around Riley's shoulder. She looked him over, then straightened his tie. "Have I told you how hot you look today?" she asked, grinning. "Because this button-down is one of my faves. Totally appreciate Coach Collins's game day dress code."

"I'm hot either way," Tate said, "but thanks. The next time you get mad at me, remember how hot I am."

I backed away. "Right," I said, mostly to myself. "Got to go to the field house. See you two later."

"We've still got a few minutes before the bus leaves," Riley replied. "If you'll wait, I'll walk you."

"You're headed to the field house?" Adam asked, coming to a stop beside me. "Great. I needed someone to annoy me on the way." I frowned, but he didn't seem to notice or care. "Tate, hurry up. If you're late to the bus, it won't be good."

"Be there in a few," Tate said.

Adam nodded and loosely rested his hand on my shoulder. It wasn't until we entered the warm afternoon air that I mustered the nerve to say something.

"Why are you being so weird?" I asked, facing him. He arched an eyebrow, and I shrugged. "You haven't said a word to me all day, and you keep staring at me instead of acting like your normal jerkish self. What's up? What's your problem?"

"I don't have a problem," he answered. "I'm in a good mood today. Be thankful and move on." He stopped beside his truck and opened the back door. He tossed his letter jacket and backpack onto the leather seat. "Besides," he added, closing the door, "it's game day. I need to focus on things like plays and team dynamics. That's hard to do if I spend my day talking to you. You've cornered the market on nagging."

"The only time I nag is when you deserve it."

"Plus anytime you're bored," he replied.

"That too."

A breeze sifted through the humid air. It whipped brown waves against my cheeks and sent Adam's messy hair into his eyes. He raked a hand through it and glanced at a set of students who told him good luck at tonight's game.

"Thanks," he answered.

At the field house, a banner from the pep rally puffed in the wind. Adam poked it with his finger before opening the large metal door.

"Thanks, Meade," I said, stepping through. "That was very gentlemanly of you."

"I try."

Excitement charged the weight room, amplified by football players who hauled duffel bags and equipment in and out the door. In the hall, the entrance to the locker room was wedged open and decorated with pirate gear. Adam ducked below a low-hung pirate flag on his way inside.

I continued to the coach's office, where my dad stood behind his desk, fiddling with a briefcase. He raised concerned eyes, but breathed a sigh of relief when I passed through the door.

"You made it on time!" he said.

"On time for what?" He shot me a smile as sweet as syrup, and I shook my head. "Nope," I said. "Not doing anything football related."

"But I need a favor from my favorite daughter."

"I'm your only daughter. Quit pretending I'm your favorite."

"Twenty bucks?"

"Pretend all you want." I crossed the room and took the clipboard extended my way. A detailed spreadsheet was clipped to the top, broken into sections marked rushing, passing, and receiving. "You want me to keep stats?" I asked. "Who are you, and what did you do with my dad?"

"Don't worry, we're taping the game, too." He closed his briefcase and slung the strap over his shoulder. "Love you, but we both know you're easily distracted. I don't want a repeat of last time."

"There was a UFO, and I was documenting it for NASA," I explained.

"How could I forget? You drew a picture of it when you were supposed to be watching the game."

"That picture was a detailed diagram of the ship and should've been sent to the president," I said. "There could've been an alien race named after me."

"You'd also be the newest resident of the state's insane asylum," he said.

He handed me a football shirt, and I looked it over. "Trying to change the topic with free clothes? Smooth, Dad. Very smooth."

"And highly effective," he said. He stepped from behind his desk and moved toward the door. "If you do a good job, maybe I'll bribe you to stay on as a full-time manager."

"No thanks."

He flipped the lights, and I followed him into the hall. When players continued to file in and out of the locker room, he poked his head through the door. "Bus. Five minutes!" he hollered. "If we're late, you'll owe me quads on Monday."

The remaining stragglers clutched their duffels and sprinted through the door. My dad chuckled as we moved toward the exit. "Knew that would work."

Outside, beneath the afternoon sun, a school bus was parked beside the building. Loud conversations carried through a few open windows, but the bus fell silent as my dad and I stepped inside.

My nose scrunched at the overwhelming smell of cologne, body wash, and sweaty cleats. The scent's intensity was magnified by humidity and hung in the bus like a thick, suffocating cloud. If I was lucky, the odor wouldn't seep into my clothes. If it did, I'd catch whiffs until I could shower.

I slid into the seat behind the driver and grimaced as my legs stuck to the vinyl. Had I known I'd be on a bus, I would've worn jeans. There were few things more cringeworthy than being stuck to a nasty bus seat.

My dad dropped his briefcase in the seat beside me and tugged a Pader High hat over his hair. He stood at the front, serious as he surveyed the team.

"Hello, gentlemen," he said. "Today is a good day for football. On the ride over there, I want you to think about one thing—how everything we've done has led us here. I want you to think about every drop of sweat you've shed, every drop of blood you've bled out on that field. We've worked, we've run, we've done everything we can to be able to get out on that field tonight and walk away knowing that we gave it everything we got.

"Now, I know this is just another first game day for some of you. You might have another year, maybe two, but for some of my seniors, this is it. I want you to let that soak in for a minute. I want you to think about everything you've worked for the last three years. How every practice, every sprint you've run, every weight you've lifted, has led you here. You are my leaders, and I know you'll lead us tonight.

"Let's go out there and start this season right. When you walk out on that field, strive for perfection. Go out there and give it everything you've got. Win or lose, that'll be enough for me.

"On the count of three. One, two, three . . . Pader!"

* * *

Football players, with blades of grass stuck beneath their cleats and jerseys plastered to their bodies, carried the smell of dirt and sweat across the locker room's threshold. Exhausted and sore, Pader's football team stood in the middle of the locker room. Football had worn them down, but they did exactly what they planned.

My dad took his place at the front of the room, a football in his hand and a smile pasted on his face. When he shot the team a thumbs-up, their cheers echoed off the lockers around them. Players jumped and knocked into each other, then turned and gave high fives.

Even I, Football Scrooge, had the urge to beat my hand against the locker in celebration. My palm stung as it landed flat against the metal. Case laughed at me as I shook out the sting. Stupid doors.

"All right!" my dad said, clapping his hand against the football. "Great game! Can't think of a better way to start district." He motioned for my clipboard and took it with his free hand. After a quick glance, he lifted his attention. "We need to work on the veer, but I have full confidence. We'll look at the specifics tomorrow during film. Next thing: game ball." He extended the ball in front of him. Players watched as he swept it across the room. "With four touchdowns and two hundred total yards, tonight's MVP is Mr. Tate Mack."

The boys erupted into hoots and hollers as my dad tossed Tate the football.

"Keep playing like that, and you'll be signing a letter of intent in the spring," he said.

Tate rolled the ball in his hands and smiled. "Thanks, Coach! Means a lot."

"It was well earned," my dad replied. He handed the clipboard to one of his assistants and checked his watch. "All right. Get changed, check the locker room, and get on the bus. We're leaving in ten. Meade, a word when you're done?"

"Yes, Coach."

My dad moved through the door, and I exited at his side. He glanced at me and pulled his phone from his pocket while the other coaches continued down the hall.

"Thinking about the diner on the outskirts of town," he said. "Concerns about potential food poisoning? You're a better restaurant judge than me."

"Looked good," I replied. "Can we order cheeseburgers? I need meat."

"Possibly. The school only gave me five bucks a person, so I'll have to check the price." He punched in a number on his cell and moved out of earshot as players exited the locker room. "Bus," he told them.

Their dress shoes squeaked against the concrete while my

dad returned to the call. Instead of following the players, I leaned against the bricks and fidgeted with a loose string on the hem of my shirt. I wanted cheeseburger assurance from the source and was too impatient to wait until he got on the bus.

A throat cleared behind me. I glanced over my shoulder to find Adam strolling through the locker room door. With damp hair curled at the ends, sleeves rolled to his elbows, and a tie hung loosely around his neck, he leaned against the bricks and stared at me.

"Your dad on the phone?" he asked.

"Yeah. He's calling about food."

Adam's arm grazed mine and heat poured across my skin. He was like a fire, lit by football and fanned by victory. He wouldn't cool down until the win wore off. Seth was the same.

Case exited the locker room in the next string of guys. He looked at Adam before looking at me. "What's Dad doing?" he asked, stopping beside us.

"Ordering food," I replied.

Case nodded and sipped from a water bottle. "Thought the players were supposed to head to the bus," he said to Adam. "Did I miss something or is that still the plan?"

"I'm waiting on your dad," Adam answered. "Thought I'd flirt with your sister while I waited. That good with you?"

Case choked on his water, and my cheeks flamed.

"Just thought I'd be honest," Adam continued. "Why beat around the bush, right?"

"Right." Case cocked his jaw and hesitated before taking a step back. "Just know that if you hurt my sister, I'll hurt you. You'll be in the hospital for days."

I pinched the bridge of my nose and tried to cover my embarrassment. All I got in return was Adam's amused laugh as Case continued down the hall.

"Don't think he expected that answer," Adam said.

"Neither of us did." I pushed a strand of hair behind my ear and shot Adam a challenging smile. "But I'd rather gouge my eyes out than flirt with you. You're barking up the wrong tree, Sparky."

"We'll see," he answered, grinning.

"Burgers ordered!" My dad stopped beside me and waved his phone. "Ordered fries, too. You're welcome. Hopefully, everything will be done before we get there." He crammed his phone in his pocket and nodded toward the exit. "Meet you at the bus, Claire? I need to talk to Adam."

"Okay."

I pulled myself away from the wall and caught the faint murmur of "football trip" as I walked to the door.

Outside, grass glowed beneath stadium lights. The stands had cleared, but the players' conversations lingered in the dark. Their voices grew louder as grass morphed into loose gravel. The bus sat alone at the back of the parking lot, and I earned the temporary attention of the team as I made my way inside and found my seat behind the driver.

Case glanced at me but was caught in a conversation with a few of his teammates. He had to postpone his interrogation on my social life, but I knew to expect it within a few days. He'd want info about Adam I wasn't willing to give.

The back of my legs sat flush against the vinyl as I pulled my phone from my pocket and relaxed against the window. My Facebook and Twitter feeds were filled with game day pictures from all my old friends. They won their game, too, and I was happy for them, but I should've been there. My eyes burned as I landed on a picture of Seth. Clad in a navy-and-gold jersey, he had his arm wrapped around a cheerleader's shoulder—a new cheerleader. When I spotted the blue bracelet wrapped around her wrist, identical to the one on mine, jealousy swept through me. I'd been replaced by Claire 2.0!

"Who's that?" Adam asked, sliding into the seat beside me. I glared at him over the screen. "Let me try again. Hi. Who's the dick face on your phone screen?"

"No one," I grumbled.

I shut off the screen and rubbed my temples with my hand. A ball of anger swelled in my throat, threatening to spill over and drown me in emotion. This wasn't the time or place to lose it over Seth. If nothing else, it gave Adam more ammunition to tease me.

"Go rejoin the land of your people," I told him, turning so I faced the window.

"Last time I checked, you don't own the bus," he replied.

My dad boarded the bus, and it pulled out of the parking lot onto a busy road. Adam relaxed beside me, his eyes in my direction as we crossed through town.

"Rumor has it you're going to the lake with us tomorrow," he said. "Any truth to that rumor?"

"I don't know."

"Okay, but are you leaning more toward yes or no?" he asked. "I'm in charge of drinks, and I need to know how much to bring. If I don't bring enough, I'll end up sharing my Gatorade with you. Sorry, but I don't want to share."

"I don't know," I repeated.

He frowned. "Someone's grumpy."

"Sure am, Snow White."

Through the window, building silhouettes weaved between tall trees. I focused on them and tried to control my breathing. The sooner I could calm myself, the better.

"So, you're not going to talk to me at all?" Adam asked.

"Nope," I answered.

He shrugged and crossed his arms. He remained in the same position as the bus stopped at the diner. He didn't move until there was food on the bus.

The smell of charbroiled patties drew my focus. My mind was on a million other things, but I wasn't resistant to the tantalizing aroma of grilled beef. My dad handed a set of brown paper bags to Adam and continued toward the back.

"Too bad these aren't vegetarian," Adam said, holding my food out of reach.

"Give me my burger, or I'll claw your eyes out."

"Kinky."

I reached for my bag, but he refused to give it to me.

"These are acrylic and extremely effective in inflicting bodily harm," I said, flashing my sparkly black fingernails. "If you don't want me to scar your money maker, give me my burger now."

He handed me the bag, and I ripped into the contents. Staring back at me was a much-needed, greasy cheeseburger.

"Is that your way of saying I'm hot?" he asked, opening a ketchup packet.

"You were granted the gift of beauty to make up for your lack of intelligence," I answered.

Ketchup flew all over my shirt. I glared at Adam. "Tell me that was an accident," I grumbled. "It better have been an accident."

Adam gave me a sheepish smile and flashed a half-filled packet of ketchup. "Whoops. Butterfingers."

"I'll give you a finger."

My dad returned to his seat, and the bus left the diner parking lot. I kept a wary eye on the condiments. When we finally merged onto the highway, I decided it was safe to shift my gaze. I slathered the burger in mayo, decided it wasn't enough, and stole two discarded packets from Adam's bag.

He watched me, amused, as I finished soaking the patty. "Want some burger with your mayo?" he asked as I lifted the burger to my mouth. I discreetly flipped him off, and he laughed. "Not judging, but you infringed on my condiments."

I rolled my eyes and took another bite. Adam was staring at me and wouldn't look away. "Quit looking at me," I said, shifting in the seat. "It's weird, and I want to eat my burger in peace."

"I'm looking out the window. Quit being so self-absorbed."

"You calling me self-absorbed is funny," I replied. "It's like you took your biggest personality trait and tossed it on me."

"Or, I identified *your* biggest personality trait and brought it to your attention."

"You know what, asshole—"

Adam's hand landed over my mouth, and he pointed at my dad. "Don't know how your parents are about cursing, but my grandma loses her shit. Cool it."

"Yes, Mom."

His eyes narrowed as he sat his burger on my lap. I looked at it, trying to register how I'd become Adam Meade's tray table.

"Um, my lap," I said.

"Deal with it." He reached for the duffel lying on the floor. When he straightened, he held a bottle of Gatorade in one hand

and a bottle of water in the other. "Here," he said, handing me the water.

"Is there a catch?" I asked, taking it.

"What makes you think there'd be a catch?"

"Figured I'd ask."

Adam retrieved his burger and adjusted the bun. "Sometimes you should just say thank you and move on. Life is too short to be skeptical of people."

"Been around a lot of people," I answered. "If I'm skeptical, it's for a reason."

"What's the reason?"

I shook my head. That was a long conversation, centered on Seth. I wasn't talking about it tonight.

Adam surveyed me, quiet as he munched on his food. "Whatever it is," he said, crumpling the wrapper, "forget it. I don't beat around the bush. I give you something, it's because I want to. No catch. No strings attached."

"You sure about that, Meade?"

"Positive."

Hit On

Wood creaked beneath my feet, disturbing the silent living room. I stood in an unfamiliar house, with little to defend myself, but I had to try. If I didn't, the mouse would swallow me whole.

The rodent turned. Its beady black eyes menaced me through the dark. In one swift move, it charged. My spine collided with the counter, and I raised my hands to defend myself. I could fight it. I had to fight it, or I'd never make it home alive.

"Come and get me!" I screamed, swinging my fists at it.

Whack!

"Son of a bitch!"

My eyes flickered open. I blinked against the bus's interior light. Adam sat on my right, clutching his jaw as the last of his teammates stepped on the gravel outside.

"Why did you hit me?!" he griped. "Here I am, trying to be a nice guy, and you thanked me with a right hook!" He stood, livid, and moved his jaw left to right. "Damn, you hit hard!"

"I was fighting a mouse," I croaked, straightening in the seat.

"News flash: You weren't." He tossed his duffel over his shoulder and winced. "I told your dad I'd wake you up. No wonder he was so quick to accept."

"Kicked him in the groin before," I muttered. "I was thirteen. He was on the floor for ten minutes." Adam's scowl morphed into fear. "I have vivid dreams," I defended. "It's not like I can help it."

"Clearly."

He stepped toward the exit, a red spot visible against his jaw.

"You should ice that," I said, collecting my things. "It'll bruise if you don't."

"It'll bruise either way."

He exited the bus, and I followed. Gravel crunched and scattered beneath his harsh strides.

"It was an accident!" I said, catching him as he entered the field house.

"Sure it was."

He was a ninja in the dark, navigating the machines with ease. When he entered the hallway, the spot where I punched him became easier to see. At this rate, it would be bruised by morning.

Regret swirled as I tried to hold his pace. "I promise it was an accident," I said. "I didn't mean to hit you."

Adam pushed his way into the locker room and was immediately hidden by the thick aluminum door that separated us.

I sighed and leaned my back against the wall. Cold seeped through my football T-shirt, sending goose bumps up my arms.

The air-conditioner vents turned the hall frigid, but they wouldn't compare to Adam. One day of being ignored was enough to know I didn't want him to freeze me out. My only option was to make this right.

I was still leaning against the wall when the door swung open. Adam paused in the doorway. "You're kidding me," he groaned.

"Think of me as Claire the Ice Fairy."

"What about Claire the Perpetual Pain in My Ass?"

"Shut up." I grabbed his hand and pulled him down the hall. "I'm trying to apologize. Let me."

"I don't need your apology."

I pushed my way into the training room and reeled from the arctic temperatures inside. I swore at the ice machine for being both a blessing and a curse and directed Adam to a large metal table on the other side.

"Sit your butt over there and wait," I said. "I'll be with you in a minute."

"(A) Don't tell me what to do. (B) I need to get home. I have things to do and people to see. You aren't one of them."

I ignored him and opened a supply cabinet. Adam plopped onto the table. The metal creaked beneath his weight as he scooted to the edge.

"See," he said. "Even the table is protesting."

"Tell the table to mind its own business."

With a quart-sized bag in hand, I found the ice machine. My fingers turned rosy as I scooped the ice inside.

"You don't have to do this," Adam said. "I'm fine. It isn't the first time I've gotten hit in the face. Doubt it will be the last. I promise it'll heal."

I dropped the lid with a thud and zipped the bag. When I stopped in front of Adam, I motioned to his face. "Let me see it."

"No."

I ignored him and gingerly put my hand beneath his jaw. Stubble scraped my fingers as I tilted it for a better view.

"I'm fine," he repeated.

"And now you'll be better." I pushed the bag flush against his skin, and he pulled back.

"That's cold!"

"Freezing," I said. I kept the bag firm against his face, despite his objections. "If it wasn't cold, this would be a waste of time."

"It's a waste of time regardless." He huffed and raised his hand to the bag, covering mine with calloused fingers and a warm touch. "If you would've kept your hands to yourself, none of this would've happened."

"You should've made my dad wake me up," I countered.

His green eyes flickered across my face, surveying me quietly. I returned the stare with equal intensity. We waited for the other to crack, neither looking away.

"Where did you learn to hit like that?" he asked.

"My dad." I shifted my palm against the ice and shrugged. "He figured I should know how to defend myself. Since I'm always around guys, I thought he was probably right. Never know when one of you might do something stupid."

"Fair enough," Adam said. He let his thumb run across the top of my hand. His fingers left a trail of nerves in their wake. "You always been around football?"

"For the most part." I pulled my hand from beneath his and

let him hold the ice. "My dad started coaching when I was in kindergarten."

"Have you moved around a lot?"

"Six times."

"Is this your favorite school?"

"Is this twenty questions?"

"Answer the question, Collins," he said, smiling. "It's the least you can do for hitting me."

"Fine," I said, rolling my eyes. "It isn't my favorite school."

"Didn't think so," he replied. "Not that I blame you. Had to be pretty shitty, moving here your senior year."

"It was."

He nodded and let out a slow exhale. "And that was what you were looking at on the bus, wasn't it? Your old friends? Old boyfriend?"

Emotions knotted in my throat. "That's none of your business."

"Is that a yes?"

I shook my head and pivoted.

"Just trying to get to know you," he said.

"Save yourself the trouble."

"Hey." He tossed the bag on the counter and caught me beside the ice machine. "You seemed upset on the bus, so I figured it was a pretty good guess. I wasn't trying to upset you."

"If you don't want to upset me, don't bring it up. Ask me my favorite color. Ask me my favorite food." I swallowed a lump in my throat and shook my head. "Ask me whatever you want, but don't ask about my old school. It's personal."

"I was just trying to get to know you," he repeated, his tone soft.

"Why?"

"Because I want to."

An invisible weight settled on my chest. Adam continued to stare, his expression the same unreadable one he'd worn all day. He looked caught between words and silence. I decided the route instead.

"Quit looking at me like that," I said.

"Like what?"

"That." I pointed at his face. "You get this look, like you're torn between what to do and what not to do, and it makes your brow squish together."

"Well, if you were easier to read, I wouldn't have to make that face. Blame yourself." He poked me in the middle of the forehead, and I batted him away. "Don't like my looks? Don't bring them upon yourself."

"I don't bring them upon myself," I said.

"Yeah, you do," he said, eyes narrowing as he scanned my face. "You're the only girl I know who can be around me and not care who I am or what I look like. I don't like it. It's a blow to my ego and confusing as hell."

"Good."

"Not good," he argued. "I like knowing where I stand. You give me nothing but sarcasm and snarky remarks. What's a guy supposed to do with that? How am I supposed to figure out if you despise me or like me or both?"

"You're the same," I said. "Sometimes you're an asshole. Other times you're decent. I don't know how to read you, either."

"Then quit trying to read me," he said. "If you want to know something, ask. It's not like I'm an ass all the time. There's a small margin when I'm fairly likeable and genuine."

"And when is that margin? When you're sleeping?"

"Plus government class," he said. "Occasionally lunch, but it depends on the food being served."

A smile found its way to my face. Adam smiled back.

"I'll make a mental note," I answered.

"You do that."

He towered over me, a shield of heat against the cold. His body was close to mine. The buttons of his shirt pressed against my T-shirt's thin fabric. His presence encompassed my senses, made my nerves stand on end, and shut off all reasonable thought to my brain. I was useless, lost to Adam's tall frame and the smell of men's deodorant that rose off him.

My cheeks burned as strands of his hair brushed my forehead, subdued only by the chill that tingled up my spine as Adam's hand pressed against my lower back.

He had that stupid look again. My heart sped.

"Next time you want to know what I'm thinking, ask me," he said, his voice low. "If I like you enough, I might tell you what it is."

"What are you thinking now?" I answered.

"Something I shouldn't."

His breathing slowed as he leaned closer, closing the distance between us. The training room's door flew open.

"There you are! I thought you—" My dad froze, his brow furrowed as he looked from me to Adam. Slowly, his lips spread into a thin line. "Meade," he said, cocking his head to the side. "Thought you went home. Everything all right?"

"Yes, sir." Adam shifted his weight and grabbed the ice from the counter. "I . . . uh . . . I was leaving. I needed this. Claire hit on me."

My eyes widened. Adam's face paled.

"I mean, she hit me," he corrected. "She punched me in the jaw."

My dad nodded. "Yep. That's definitely how it looked."

Adam placed the bag to his jaw and moved through the room. "Okay," he said, reaching the door. "The two of you have a nice night."

"Bye," my dad answered.

Adam exited the room as if it were on fire, but my cheeks were the only thing that burned. Thank everything in the world my dad waited until the door closed before he spoke.

"Something you want to tell me, Claire?"

I shook my head. "Nope. I hit him and was getting him ice."

"Hit *on* him, you mean?"

I used my hand to shield my dad from view. He was still laughing when we exited the field house. Humidity clung to my skin as I crossed the gravel toward his large white truck.

"It's fine," he said, unlocking the doors. "My rules for dating are simple. No drinking, no drugs, no wrecking the car, and no getting anyone pregnant."

"It was only ice," I repeated, my hand curling around the handle before I pulled the door open.

"Sure it was," he answered, "but we'll get your mom's take on the matter."

I was standing on the running board when his words soaked in. "You're going to tell Mom," I groaned.

"Absolutely," he replied. "Right down to the time and place of the incident." I hung my head, and he grinned. "Don't worry. Adam's a heck of a football player and a pretty stand-up guy. Much better than your last boyfriend."

I flinched at the mention of Seth and caught sight of the

Auburn bracelet around my wrist. Feelings, conflicted by every-thing the night brought, tore their way through me and buried themselves in my gut.

"It would be better if she didn't know," I replied, letting my fingers trace the bracelet's rubber facing. "It was nothing. Really."

"When she's pestering you, she isn't pestering me," my dad answered. "Besides, it'll provide hours of entertainment, and I'll be spared the consequences of not telling her. It's for the best."

"I don't believe you."

"I don't expect you to." He put the key in the ignition, and the soft strum of classic country drifted through the speakers. "Now buckle up. We have a story to tell."

"I don't want to," I whined.

"Great! I'll do the honors."

Keep It Simple

"Your dad was seeing things?"

"Yes. He made the whole thing up." I clipped the stems on a batch of roses and shoved them in an iridescent vase. My mom's skeptical side-eye didn't go unnoticed. "I blame his old age," I continued. "Short-term memory is the first to go."

"He's only a year older than me," she replied.

"Then I guess you're up next."

I carried the vase across the room and sat it next to the others. My mom's blue eyes followed me as I walked.

"Sure *your* memory isn't the problem?" she asked, occupying herself with ribbon.

"It was an ice pack and a *have a good night*," I answered. "Pretty hard to mix that up."

"Then why were you standing by the ice machine with your faces pushed together?"

"They weren't pushed together!" I threw my hands up and scowled. "You know what? Never mind. I need to head out before I'm late."

"Right," she agreed. "Go join Adam at the lake. Try not to kiss him again."

"Mom." I rubbed my temples and willed her nosiness away. "Can I borrow some money?"

She leaned across the counter, amused. "First you refuse to give me the details. Then you use me for money?"

"No one said parenting would be easy."

She grinned and motioned to her brown leather bag. "Fine, go enjoy your day in the sun. I'll be here, trying to practice on these without losing all feeling in my fingers. I've stabbed myself so many times I've lost count."

I glanced at the ribbons sprawled across the counter. A few were pinned together, but none of it looked organized. "What are those?" I asked, grabbing her purse.

"Ribbons," she answered. "I started getting preorder calls for Homecoming. Had no clue what they were talking about, so I asked around. There's this tradition called pinning. Big deal, from what I'm told."

"Interesting," I said, retrieving a twenty.

"Yep." She snipped the end of a ribbon, watching me as I returned her purse. "You should ask Adam if he wants me to make you one. I'll give him the family discount."

"Bye now."

"We can do customized!"

"Bye!" I repeated.

The blue Cruze Case and I shared was parked in the lot. When I opened its door, heat fled from inside. A vanilla air freshener hung from the rearview mirror, faded by the sun that hammered it each day. It whipped in the air-conditioning as I put the car in drive.

Halfway to the lake, my phone rang. I hit a button on the steering wheel and glanced at the clock. Riley echoed what I already knew.

"You're late."

"I know," I answered. "Driving there as we speak." Music played in the background and mixed with Adam's and Tate's deep drawls. "Are you already on the boat?"

"The guys just got it unloaded," she replied. "No biggie. We'll wait until you get here."

"It *is* a biggie," Adam argued. "By the time we get to our spot, all the good fish will be gone!" I heard a substantial *smack*. "I'm kidding!" he said. "Hands to yourself, or I'll toss you overboard."

"Toss her overboard, and you'll be sitting on the dock, watching us sail away," Tate answered.

"Traitor."

"The map says ten minutes," I said, passing Steele Creek. "I'll be there as soon as I can."

"Okay."

I hit the END CALL button and changed lanes. Twelve minutes later, I passed the blue WELCOME TO SOUTH CAROLINA sign. The marina wasn't far. Adam's black truck stuck out like a sore thumb in a mostly empty parking lot. I parked beside it, shrugged a tote over my shoulder, and closed the door.

Sitting at the dock, rocking against murky blue waves that moved with the wind, was a medium-sized pontoon boat. Riley stood behind its radio, waving at me as I closed the distance.

"Glad you found it," she said, extending a hand for my bag.

"Same."

I handed her the tote as Tate leaned across the side and pulled the boat flush against the dock. My hand wrapped around the metal siding, and I stepped on board, wobbling momentarily before I adjusted to the water.

The scent of sunblock combined with the smell of the lake, carrying summertime memories that I quickly pushed away. Today would be a good one, no matter what.

"Look who finally showed up," Adam said, earning my attention.

He wore sunglasses and a black cap. His biceps glistened in the sun, tan with undertones of pink. Lean muscles rippled over his abdomen. Scars littered his chest like nicks in armor—pale slices that marred his skin. The largest scar carved a jagged line above his swim trunks and extended to his left hip.

He snapped his fingers in my face. "Hey. Eyes up here."

I cleared my throat and tried to cover my embarrassment by busying myself with my bag. It didn't matter. Adam caught me red-handed, and he knew it.

He chuckled and adjusted his hat before plopping into a chair at the front. "Can we go?" he asked. "Or is someone else running fifteen minutes late?"

"You hush," Riley scolded.

She sashayed over to me, her head bobbing with the pop music that played through the speakers. Her pink-and-white bikini was a stark contrast from my black two-piece. She was Beach Barbie, and I was Wednesday Addams.

She pulled a large sun hat from the seat and dropped beside me. "I'm ready for the water," she commented. "Bring on the tan."

"Have fun," I answered. I pulled a pocket folder from my tote and flashed it her way. "I'm working on scholarship essays. Yay, college."

"We have a whole afternoon on the lake," she said. "Wait until we get back, and I'll help you fill them out."

"Can't. They have to be completed by me."

"They have to be dictated by you," she corrected. "Think of me as your personal scribe." She motioned for the folder, but I clung to it. "It's for your own good. Give me the folder."

"No."

"Give her the folder," Adam said.

I glared at him. He was sprawled across his chair, the sun beating down on his bare chest and his long legs extended so his ankles rested on the side of the boat. He looked so hot, he put the sun to shame.

"Not everyone has football to rely on," I answered.

He tilted his face from its upward position and stared at me. "What does that mean?"

"It means you might have a football scholarship waiting on you, but I don't. I have to get these done, and I have to get them done today. The folder stays with me."

"Downer."

"Meathead."

He chuckled and looked at the sky. "Fine. Fill out your papers. Riley, go bug Tate instead."

"Don't tell her to bug *me*!" Tate said.

Adam only laughed louder.

We passed miles of pebbled beach, but Tate didn't stop the boat until we entered a secluded cove. Trees skimmed the banks, and their leaves rippled murky water where turtles bobbed through the surface. For the day, this was our own little slice of the world. It grew quiet as Tate and Adam anchored the boat and busied themselves with fishing rods.

"Tate," Riley said, opening the door to a compartment in the back. "Do you know where the rafts are?"

"They're in the other one," he replied.

She padded barefoot across the boat's gray floor and returned to Tate with a pair of deflated inner tubes. Tate looked at her, pouted at his fishing reel, and handed it to Adam. Ten minutes later, both tubes were inflated and tied to the boat. They floated on the water like two neon doughnuts in a pool of muddy blue.

"You coming?" she asked me, arching an eyebrow as she moved toward the boat's metal steps.

"Scholarships," I answered, waving the folder back and forth.

She frowned and pointed at the floats. I frowned and pointed at the folder.

"Make Tate go," Adam said, tugging his cap lower on his brow. Tate looked at him wide-eyed, and he grinned. "You heard me. Go spend quality time with your girlfriend. You can fish after."

"Yeah, Tate!" Riley said. "Come with me!"

"There's no way I'm getting in that water," Tate answered.

"Wuss," Adam replied.

Tate scowled and crossed his arms in front of his chest.

"We won't be back at the lake until next year," Riley said. "Even then, it won't be often. Come on. Come float with me while you still can."

"I don't want to," he said.

"Please, Tate."

He sighed and nodded. "I'll float with you for ten minutes, but if one turtle bites my butt, I'm done."

"Yes!"

The boat shook as they moved toward the stern. I waited for things to mellow, then rested the folder against my lap and sifted through various Auburn scholarship applications. Adam took one from the stack and wore a neutral expression as he scanned the words.

"Between this, the magnets in your locker, and that bracelet around your wrist, I assume you want to go to Alabama."

"Give it back," I answered. "It's rude to take other people's stuff."

"Sorry, manners police." He handed me the paper and crossed his arms. "Why do you want to go to Alabama? Family alma mater?"

"It isn't Alabama, it's Auburn, and it's none of your business."

"Auburn is in Alabama. Therefore, you want to go to Alabama." He shifted his weight. "Also, do you remember the conversation we had last night? The one where I said I was trying to get to know you? That's what this is. Answer. Please."

"Remember when I told you I don't want to talk about personal things? This falls under that category." I resumed my attention to the application, but he took a seat beside me and put his hand over the form. "If I can't see the words, I can't write a response," I groaned. "Move your hand."

"Talk to me and I will." I narrowed my eyes at him, and he smiled. "At least let me address you almost kissing me last night. I feel like we left on an awkward note, and it's bugging the hell out of me."

I knocked his hand out of the way but maintained my stare. "It was an almost kiss," I answered. "Had it been more than that, a conversation would be needed."

"Good. Glad we're in agreement."

He relaxed into the seat and played with his cap. I couldn't see his eyes, but they burned holes in my face.

"Anything else you need?" I asked. "I can't work on these when you're looking at me like that."

"Yeah," he answered. "We need to talk about one more thing, and you may not like what I have to say."

"Try me."

"Okay." He nodded and exhaled. "We've got a good thing going," he started, motioning at Tate and Riley. "The three of us get along, have fun, and have each other's backs. Last night, I almost screwed that up. This can't happen. You and I can't happen. I've got too much to do this year, and I don't have time for a girlfriend. It's too much drama."

I closed my folder before the papers blew away. "So, I'm a threat to your busy year because I'm full of drama?" I asked, cocking my head to the side. "Or because you aren't interested, but you think I am?"

He leaned forward and clasped his hands together. "I don't know if you're interested or not, but it doesn't matter. We graduate in nine months. I need to focus on football. College scouts, recruiting trips, a full ride to the school of my choice—those are the important things. I won't waste my senior year on a relationship that has no future, and I won't jeopardize football for a girl. I'm not that kind of guy. It's that simple, and it has nothing to do with you. Don't think you did anything wrong."

"How honorable," I grumbled.

It was the same type of bull Seth gave me when he ended our relationship, and it shouldn't have pissed me off, but it did. Everything always came down to excuses. At least Adam was honest now instead of later. I guess I could respect him for that.

"Let's keep this simple," Adam said. "We can do the friend thing, but don't overcomplicate it. It's easier this way."

"I can keep it simple," I agreed, shifting my eyes to the folder.

"Good," he answered. "We'll keep it simple."

Propositions

"Let me borrow the car."

"No."

Case leaned against my locker, a scowl on his face. "But you haven't given me the keys in three weeks," he protested. "I was cool about your date with Meade, and with you taking the car to the lake, but it's my turn. Give me the keys, or I'm telling Mom."

"The last time you borrowed the car, you left the gas on empty, and I had to trade Mom manual labor for money. Until the tank runs out, the car is mine."

"This is messed up," he argued.

"Feel free to nominate me for villain of the year."

I closed my locker and moved toward government. Case held my stride.

"You're staying with Riley after the game," he said. "There's no reason why you need the car when she can take you wherever you need to go."

"Maybe I like having my own form of transportation."

"Or maybe you like being a car hog who keeps her little brother from enjoying his social life," Case groaned. He gripped my forearm and spun me in my tracks. "It's Homecoming, Claire. If you'll let me borrow the car, I'll make sure there's gas in the tank."

"And you'll do my chores for a week?" I asked.

"Three days."

"Five."

"Four."

I nodded. "Four days and a full tank of gas. You have yourself a deal." I pulled the keys from my backpack and handed them to him, then patted him on the shoulder as I continued. "FYI, Mom's making enchilada casserole on Sunday. Good luck scraping the burned stuff off the pan."

"Whoa, whoa, whoa. Hold up—"

I ignored his horrified expression. Mom's enchilada casserole was the most disgusting food on the planet, but if he would've checked the menu on the fridge, he would've known better than to take me up on the offer. Now it was too late to back out.

Government was full when I got there. When I found my seat, Adam was already seated behind me, chatting with a girl a few rows from mine. I tuned him out. We hadn't spoken much since that day at the lake, and it was easier to ignore the awkwardness between us when I didn't acknowledge him at all.

Overhead, the bell's shrill cry flooded the room. Adam relaxed in his seat, and I finished unloading my stuff.

"You were almost late," he said.

I looked back, trying to figure out who he was talking to. Me.

"Maybe I should get you a watch for Christmas," he continued, grinning. "It'll help with time management."

I flashed him my expensive birthday gift. "I have a watch, but you can get me a black one to match your heart."

"Funny."

"I know."

The room quieted as our professor appeared on the television screen. I unloaded my backpack and missed the page number in the process. When I turned to look at Adam's book, he pulled it away.

"Really?" I said. "Give me the page number."

"You were mean. Ask somebody else." I gawked at him, and he mirrored my expression. "Learn to be nice to people, and maybe they'll be nice to you."

"I am nice to you," I said.

"Yeah, as nice as an ant is before it crawls into my jockstrap and bites me on the balls." I grabbed the pencil off my desk and tossed it at him. He caught it easily. "Truth hurts."

"I'll make you hurt." I motioned at his book, and he turned it. "Thanks."

"You're welcome."

We were almost finished with class when he asked to use my eraser. I shook my head, needing it myself.

"Claire, let me borrow it," he whisper-yelled.

I shook my head again.

"I need to erase something," he said, "and you owe me for telling you the page number. Fair is fair."

"I'm using it or I would."

He let out a long exhale, and his chair creaked. Within seconds, I felt an elbow in my side.

"Hi."

I looked to my right and found myself nose to nose with Adam. He grabbed my eraser before I realized it. I yanked it out of his hands and shook it at him. "It's not nice to take other people's things. I've already told you that."

"You did, but this is called borrowing." He attempted to recapture the eraser, but I held it firmly in my grasp. "Really?" he complained. "Are we going to play tug-of-war? I'll win." He snatched the eraser from my hand and erased the sentence scrawled on his paper.

"Give me back my private property, or I'll tell on you."

"Fine. Tell on me."

My fists clenched. I had two options: I could either throat-punch him, or I could pay attention to the information on the screen. I'd missed a slide's worth of notes already. The notes won out.

"Why do you get pleasure from provoking me when there's fifteen other people to bother?" I asked, putting my pencil to my paper. "Isn't there someone else you can bug?"

"Nope."

He squatted beside my desk and copied my notes. I finished the slide, then watched his profile as he concentrated on the words.

"You could bug Wendy Mallox," I whispered. "You two seemed to hit it off."

Adam glanced at the girl he had been talking to before class. She stole her eyes away when he caught her staring at him.

His mouth tilted up. "Been there. Done that," he answered. "It was good, but it's never happening again."

"Adam!"

"Too much info?"

The bell rang, and the class monitor turned on the lights. Adam stood and handed me the eraser. I took it from him, crammed it in my backpack with the rest of my stuff, and followed the other students out the door.

He caught me in the hall. "You going to the game tonight?" he asked.

I shook my head. "Thought I would stay home and watch reality television. It's not like I have a dad who's a coach."

"Ha. Are you ever serious?"

"Sometimes."

I stopped beside my locker and spun the lock. Adam stopped beside me.

"Shame you won't be there," he said. "I was going to ask if you'd wear my jersey, but I guess not."

Confused, I poked my head around the locker door. "Can you repeat what you just said? I thought I heard something about a jersey, but I'm pretty sure I'm wrong."

"You heard right," he replied.

My chest tightened as old memories flooded in. Me. The field. Seth. All of it flashing before my eyes, too familiar to ignore.

"You want me to wear your jersey?" I repeated.

"I want you to wear my jersey," he replied. His weight shifted to the balls of his feet, and he shrugged. "It's not a big deal. More a favor than anything."

"Care to elaborate?"

"It's tradition," he said. "For Homecoming, all football play-ers are given knockoff versions of their jersey. We're supposed to pass them out to the biggest football supporters in school."

"And you think I'm supportive?"

"No, but giving a jersey to any other girl would be a night-mare." He nodded at Wendy Mallox as she passed, then looked at me. "She got my jersey last year and has already asked me about it. When I told her I wasn't sure who would get it, she started bugging me. I don't want a shadow the rest of the year. Since you know where we stand, you're a safe bet."

"I'm your cop-out," I clarified.

"Kind of."

"Way to make a girl feel special, Meade."

I pushed away disappointment and stepped around him. Adam followed.

"If it helps, you also get a tacky Homecoming pin," he said. "They're these awful ribbons that are standard for the game. My grandma thought I had a date, so she ordered one. It's big and gaudy and horrible, and you'll be the envy of every girl in school."

"Not on my priorities list," I said. "Ask someone else."

"Can't. You're the only one who won't get attached." He moved around me and blocked my path. When I tried to slide past, he blocked me again. "If you won't do it for me, think about the poor old woman who already went out of her way to get your name inscribed."

My blood pressure rose. This wasn't happening. "Oh!" I said, my hands finding my hips. "So you already planned on me being the cop-out? I'm sorry, but what gave you that moronic idea?"

"We have the same friends and occasionally hang out. Didn't think it was out of the question."

"Except you've avoided me since the lake. It's been almost three weeks, Adam. I'm surprised you remember my name."

"I'm not avoiding you now," he said, flashing a smile.

"Because you need something." I pinched the bridge of my nose to keep from getting angrier.

"So is that a yes?" Adam asked.

"Not sure," I answered. "Part of me wants to turn you down on principle."

"Don't turn me down." Adam put his hand on my shoulder and gave it a light squeeze. His fingers moved to the back of my neck and rubbed the space between my shoulders. "Think of it as our first official friend event."

"I haven't agreed to go."

"Then agree and keep both of us from being late to class," he said. He lowered his hand to his pocket and withdrew a set of keys. "The stuff is in my truck. I won't be able to see you before the game, but I'll catch you after. Okay?"

He put the keys in my hand and curled my fist around them.

"I still haven't said yes," I said, watching him as he side-stepped me and move down the hall.

"I know that look, Collins. You'll say yes."

* * *

"I like him. He has good taste."

I lifted the long end of a ribbon and let it fall against my knee. "I still don't understand why people wear these," I replied. "What's the point?"

My mom adjusted the pin and took a step back. "No idea, but they bring in good revenue. I'm not complaining."

I straightened Adam's jersey and looked at myself in the mirror. It was two sizes too big and more a dress than anything, but there was nothing I could do to change that.

"Ready?" she asked.

"Yeah."

Her keys clinked in her hands, followed by the thud of the front door as we stepped onto the porch. The glow of stadium lights could be seen from our yard. The dull yellow contrasted against the obsidian sky and made my nerves stand on end.

When we reached the stadium, parking wrapped around each block. This was tonight's main event, and Pader residents flocked to the stadium like ants at a picnic, eager for success and yearning for satisfaction.

My mom found a spot a few streets over, and we walked the rest of the way. After we were herded through the entrance, she headed to the bleachers, and I split off for the field. If I had to be here, I wanted a good view. Coach's daughter had its perks. One of the managers let me in. I caught the smell of grass and freshly washed jerseys when I stopped behind the sideline. Adam acknowledged me from beside my dad, then returned his attention to the game.

Four quarters later, what was once a decent-smelling team had turned into a legion of sweaty teenagers who were trying not to lose. It would be crushing to lose on Homecoming.

"Get him!" I shuffled down the sideline, following the water girls in an attempt to blend in.

"We're going to lose," Riley said as I stopped beside the

cheerleaders. "We've got less than two minutes to make this work. That's not enough time." She blew out a breath and put her pom-poms on her hips. "And when we lose, Tate's going to cancel the after-party. I love him, but he's a sore loser. Even winning Homecoming king couldn't ease this loss."

"We still have time," I said.

"Make the tackle!" my dad yelled when the other team ran three more yards. He clutched his clipboard to his chest, concerned like everyone else on this side of the field.

The teams lined up again, and the opposing center snapped the ball. The quarterback handed it off to a running back, who tucked it against his pads and zigzagged into our defensive line.

Whack!

"There's a fumble on the play!" the announcer relayed.

White and green mixed with red and black. When a Pader linebacker came away with the ball, our sideline erupted in cheers.

"Yes!" I said, fist-bumping Riley.

I bounced on my feet, anxious, as Adam and Tate jogged across the field with our offense. With the blow of a whistle, the clock resumed.

"Ready, hut!"

The ball was snapped into Adam's gloved hands. Our players scattered. Tate and the other receivers ran down the sidelines, the opposition hot on their heels.

Adam stayed in the pocket, waiting for the right moment.

"Run!" I yelled, spotting a lineman break free.

Adam shifted backward, trying to put distance between him and the lineman. Tate reached the end zone, but before Adam could throw the ball, the lineman grabbed his face mask and pulled him to the ground.

A flag was thrown, but one of our players was already pulling the guy off Adam.

"Hey!" my dad yelled, hitting his clipboard hard enough that I worried he'd hurt his hand.

Adam got to his feet and pushed our guy backward, ushering him to the line of scrimmage. "Face mask. On the defense. Fifteen-yard penalty. First down, Pader" came over the speakers.

Adam adjusted his white wristband as he waited for his teammates to line up, then he got under center.

"Red twenty-five. Set. Hut," he said, his voice echoing across the field.

Cleats dug into the ground, and pads clashed. Adam got the ball and stepped back, his eyes on the end zone as Tate and the other receivers sprinted downfield. They were all covered by the defense, but Tate came to an abrupt stop and curled back. Adam launched the ball. It streaked across the sky and came down in Tate's hands. He clutched it to his chest, stiff-armed his defender, and crossed the goal line as the clock hit zero.

The crowd went wild.

"Touchdown, Pirates!"

Adam shook his fist above his head. Tate found him seconds later, and the pair met with a celebratory bump midair.

"Special teams!" my dad yelled, sprinting past.

He pulled guys from the sideline, and they hurried onto the field. When they successfully completed the extra point, the sideline turned into a mosh pit.

"Pader wins, twenty-one to twenty!" the announcer confirmed.

Guys collided with each other—jumping, banging each other on the helmets, slugging each other on the arms. I attempted a side bump with one of them, but accidentally rammed my side into the player's hip pad. When I came down, my side was on fire, and my ribbon was tangled in the player's helmet.

"Ah!" I yelled.

Riley found me surrounded by players and broke into a broad grin as she made her way through. "We won!" she yelled. "We won and—" She stopped, her brow furrowed as she looked at my ribbon, then the player I was attached to. "Oh," she said.

I mouthed *help* and pointed at the ribbon. If I could keep it on the down-low, that would be great. My plan was spoiled when Adam stepped through the crowd. He paused, flickered his attention between me and the guy, then continued toward us.

"This takes clingy to a whole different level," he said.

"Just help me," I whispered.

Adam nudged the guy in the arm. "Yo. Let me see your helmet." The player turned, making me turn with him. "Now," Adam added.

The player did as he was told and tugged off his helmet. Adam handed it to Riley, who traded him her pom-poms.

"How did you manage this?" she asked.

"Talent," I replied.

Adam darted a glance around the field and gave the pompoms a shake. "That was a hell of a play," he said. "I'll be signing autographs near the locker room in five. Make sure you BYOS for a personalized one." I arched an eyebrow, and he clarified. "Bring your own Sharpie. Duh."

"Already getting a big head," Riley answered. "Let me remind you: Tate made that play. Maybe *you* should BYOS."

He whopped her on the head with a pom-pom, and she attempted to kick him in the leg.

"Missed," he said, grinning. He whopped her again and retreated as she spun all the way around. "Sorry, it slipped."

"Hit me with that pom-pom again, and you'll lose an appendage," she said.

He made a face at her, and she continued untangling me from the helmet.

"Think you'll be done anytime soon?" he asked. "I need to borrow Claire before she completely destroys that ribbon."

"The ribbon is trying to destroy *me*," I said.

Riley looped the final piece through the face mask and shot him a triumphant grin. "Patience is a virtue, Adam. Develop some."

"I have no patience, and I don't plan on getting any," he replied. He traded her pom-poms for the helmet and shoved it at the player. With no other explanation, he grabbed my hand and hauled me toward the bleachers. "Thanks for releasing the beast," he told Riley, waving at her. "We'll catch you at Tate's."

We crossed the field, grass squishing beneath my boots. People exited the stairs in thick clusters of Pader Pirate gear, each offering Adam more congratulations than I could count. He was the man of the hour, but all I was focused on was the gloved hand that held mine.

He kept his grip as we ascended the stairs. Our shoes clanked along the metal, Adam's cleats louder than mine. When we were at the fifty-yard line, he leaned over. His breath was warm against my cheek, and my nerves stood on end as strands of his damp hair brushed my skin.

"Act normal," he whispered. "I know that's hard for you, but give it a go."

He straightened and continued to walk. I stuck my foot out and caught his cleat, sending him into the rail.

"How's that for normal?" I answered.

"Adam!"

Adam straightened and squeezed my hand. I squeezed his harder.

An older woman, with fluffy gray hair and eyes the same shade as Adam's, stood on the third row. Her face was warm and welcoming, etched with wrinkles that lined her mouth and surrounded her eyes. We wore the same jersey, but she had a large plastic button with Adam's picture pinned above her heart. He smiled at her as she wrapped him in a hug.

"You almost gave me a heart attack," she said. "You can't let things get that close."

"Had to keep you from falling asleep," he answered. "Your bedtime was two hours ago."

She released him and swatted him on the arm. "Now, dear. Don't forget who you live with. I might forget to leave the dead bolt unlocked. What a shame that would be."

"Wouldn't be the first time," he said. He turned and motioned at me with his free hand. "Grandma, this is Claire. Claire, this is my grandma."

"Nice to meet you, young lady," she said, pulling me in for a hug. "Wanda Meade. You may call me Grandma or Wanda, but if you call me Mrs. Meade, I'll dust your sugar cookies with salt."

"It's true," Adam said. "Tate made that mistake once."

She took a step back and winked. "And he never called me Mrs. Meade again, did he?" Adam shook his head, and she grinned.

Her attention drifted to our hands, and her grin widened. "Glad to see Adam finally brought a real date," she said. "It's about time he picked someone."

"Grandma!"

Adam's cheeks reddened, but she waved him off.

"Oh, you hush," she replied. "I'm old and senile. I can say what I want."

"Except you aren't senile," Adam answered. "You're as youthful as a spring chicken and sharper than an ax. The old people excuse doesn't fly."

"It flies if I say so." She turned and grabbed two bottles of water and a bag of Sour Patch Kids from the bleacher. "Now," she said, handing me a water before handing the rest to him. "I know you're staying at Tate's tonight, but I expect you to behave yourself. I don't want Sheriff Stevens beating down my door, explaining to me you've burnt down half the town again."

"Again?" I repeated.

Adam sighed. "In my defense, we needed something to start the bonfire. The couch was way more effective than damp wood, and it wasn't even that big."

"It was big," Wanda argued, "and your harebrained scheme got the entire town on a two-month burn ban. I don't want to explain to the girls at Scrabble Club that my grandson is involved with the law again." She scrunched her nose and looked at me. "Make sure he stays on the straight and narrow, won't you, dear?"

Adam made a comment under his breath that sounded like "I'd pay to see her try," and I nudged him in the side.

"I'll make sure he's on his best behavior," I assured her.

"Thank you, sweetie."

Adam rolled his eyes. "Yeah, yeah. Everyone loves to pick on Adam."

"Only when Adam refers to himself in the third person," Wanda said.

"You're lucky I love you." He kissed her cheek and took a step along the bleacher, tugging my hand. "We have to head out," he told her, "but call me if you need anything. If I don't answer, leave a voice mail, and I'll call you back."

"I'll be fine." She waved at us and gathered her things. "It was nice meeting you, Claire. I'm making a peach cobbler tomorrow afternoon. If the town is still standing, you should swing by and grab a piece."

"But that's my cobbler," Adam replied.

"And you can share." She shoved her stadium seat under her arm and patted him on the shoulder as she walked by. "I'll see you tomorrow. Be good."

"I will."

Wanda reached the bottom of the steps, and Adam followed her with his eyes. When she was out of sight, he looked at me.

"I love cobbler," I said.

"You stay far away."

He started back to the stairs, not bothering to let go of my hand. My common sense screamed to let go on my own, but I didn't. His hand was warm, and it wasn't like it was a big deal if I held it. It was just a hand. This was just Adam.

"Thanks for being nice to my grandma," he said, looking at me.

"I'm always nice."

I took a step toward the stairs and caught one of the long ribbons beneath my boot. Adam kept me from falling on my face, but laughed as I straightened.

"Graceful," he chuckled.

"It's this stupid ribbon," I answered. "You forgot to mention this thing was the size of Texas. That would've been a deal breaker."

"Which is exactly why I didn't tell you. You would've broken my grandma's heart and deprived me of much-needed entertainment, all in one night."

I glared at him. He thought this life-threatening decoration was entertaining? It wasn't entertaining! It had the potential to break my leg and wreck my street cred in one fell swoop.

"You're proud of yourself for sticking me with this, aren't you?" I asked, pointing at the gaudy ribbon attached to my chest.

"Yep. Thought you would've turned me down when you saw it, but here you are ribbon and all." He waved the Sour Patch Kids at me and grinned. "She was so happy, I even got these. You don't understand how much I love these things."

I studied them. "They're your favorite?"

"Sour Patch Kids are life," he replied.

"Good." I snatched the candy before he realized it and sprinted down the bleachers. "They're my favorite, too!"

10

The Truth

"I think you broke my ankle."

"Better than your heart."

Pain radiated through my leg, and I winced. Adam's lack of compassion didn't help. I pulled a bag of chips from the red-and-white tablecloth and glared at him. He returned my glare and dropped a case of water on the concrete floor.

"Besides," he said, brushing his hands against his jeans, "you missed the step. How was that my fault?"

"You were chasing me!"

"No, I was trying to get my candy back. If you wanted a piece, you should've asked."

"Would you have shared with me?" I asked.

"Nope."

I tossed a chip at him, and he chuckled as Riley crossed the barn.

"People should be here any minute," she said, her voice muffled by pop music. She wore a sequined blouse and the Homecoming queen tiara she won at the game. They gleamed in the barn's dim lighting. "Are we missing anything?" she asked. "Tate is getting ice from the house, and the DJ is set up. Food good? Plenty of drinks?"

"Everything's fine," Adam answered. He shifted around the table and sauntered to the barn's open doors.

"If everything's fine, where are you going?"

Adam paused in the threshold, annoyance written on his face. "If you must know, I'm going to check on your boyfriend. Tate's more likely to fall in the bucket than he is to hoist it into the back of my truck."

"He said he could get it on his own," she replied.

"Yeah? When has Tate ever admitted to needing help?"

"True." She looked at me, hands on her hips. "Are all guys like that?"

"As far as I know," I answered. "I chalk it up to being the inferior sex, but maybe it's just stubbornness and pride. Adam, what do you think? You've cornered the market on those traits."

He shot me the finger and ducked through the door.

I grinned and emptied another bag of chips into a bowl. Point one for Claire.

Riley grabbed a chip and munched on it. Once Adam was out of sight, she shifted her attention to me. "You two go to Homecoming together?" she asked, smiling. "Or is there a piece of the story I don't know?"

"I was a cop-out," I said, sliding the bowl across the table. "Adam was afraid another girl would get attached, so he asked me. It's not a big deal."

"Sounds like a date," she replied, smiling, "and I highly approve."

"It wasn't a date." A car pulled beside the barn, blaring country music over the rap. "People are here," I said. "Quit interrogating me and go talk to them."

"But this is way better. Do you know how long I've waited for Adam to be genuinely interested in one of my friends? Those people can wait. Give me the details."

"There's no details, Riley. This conversation is done."

"Someone's in denial."

"Someone's about to be down a friend."

A group of students stepped through the barn doors, saving me from Riley's nosiness. I recognized a few, but they immediately headed for Riley and her glittering tiara. Oh well. At least she was distracted.

My phone buzzed as I leaned against the table, listening to Riley chat with her friends. When I realized who was on the other end, a weight settled in my chest.

Seth: What are you doing?

I drifted to the back of the barn, reading and rereading the words. I hadn't heard from Seth since the calculator incident, but I hadn't tried to talk to him, either. If he didn't seem to care, why should I?

Claire: I'm at a party.
Seth: Oh.

Good. I'd leave him on *Read*.

I crammed the phone in my pocket and passed a trio of girls chatting in a small sitting area at the back. They were scattered along the hay bales, drinking from red cups while the DJ spun a beat.

"He's so incredibly gorgeous," one girl said, taking a sip.

"Hey, I called dibs!" a brunette replied.

I glanced at the DJ, a medium-build, college-aged guy Tate hired for the night. He was decent. Not worth calling dibs on, but okay to look at.

"He dropped a pencil, and I handed it to him," the brunette continued. "Even got him to say thanks."

"That's nothing," the third girl replied. "We hooked up."

"Nuh-uh," both of her friends said in unison.

The girl nodded, winking at them as she swirled her cup. "July. Right after the Fourth," she replied. "And Adam stood up to that reputation of his. Would do it again, anytime."

A sickening feeling burrowed in my stomach as the other two giggled.

"Meade has skills?" the brunette replied.

"Yep."

I stepped away, feeling the urge to throw up. Who Adam hooked up with shouldn't have affected me, but it did. I was pissed at him, and he didn't even know me in July!

The green monster of jealousy clawed at my back as I walked outside for fresh air.

Feelings were a slippery slope. Once you felt something, you felt everything else, and this felt like a sock to the gut on Christmas morning. It was a blemish on a peaceful night, a disappointment I hadn't anticipated, and exactly why we needed to keep it simple.

We were better off as friends. This was just a reminder.

* * *

"Hey, wait up!"

"Nope."

"Claire," Adam called, his voice carrying across the gravel as his pace increased. "Claire, wait up."

He caught me, but I kept my eyes on the road ahead. Behind us, the party was still in full swing. The bass pounded through the night, carried on the breeze, and the smell of smoke from Tate's fire pit swirled through the air. The party was raging, but I didn't care. I was focused on Riley and Tate, both of whom swayed like the wind and barely managed to stay upright.

"Are you ignoring me?" Adam said, his voice taking on an edge. He blocked my path, but I sidestepped him. "Okay," he continued. "Care to tell me why?"

"Nope," I answered.

He muttered under his breath and shoved his hands in his pockets. Despite seeming annoyed, he walked with me anyway.

We stopped in front of an old, abandoned building. It looked straight out of a horror film, dark, broody, and foreboding, but Tate stumbled up the cracked concrete steps, and Riley followed.

"Welcome to my humble abode," he said, extending his hands in either direction. He turned and shoved a key in the lock. "Watch your step on the way in," he continued. "Don't want anyone breaking themselves."

Riley laughed and followed him through the door. When her blond hair was shrouded by darkness, I swore. I was staying with her for the night, which meant her vehicle was the one we were taking home. Since she was drunk, it was up to me to get us there. Couldn't do that if she got lost in the haunted whatever this was.

Adam's hand wrapped around mine, and his breath grazed my cheek. "This place isn't easy to navigate. Stay with me, and you'll be fine."

"And why should I trust you?" I replied.

"Why wouldn't you?"

I kept walking, but let him hold my hand for the sake of security. If I got lost, it was better being with someone than alone. Even if it was Adam.

Inside, the room was pitch-black. People hovered close, their breath leaving them in short spurts, while Tate fiddled with something against a metal wall.

"What are we doing?" I asked Adam.

"We're playing a game," he replied.

Tate turned, a flashlight flickering on and illuminating the planes of his face. "You know the drill," he said. "Blackout hide-and-seek. Everyone from here to here is Team A. Everyone else is Team B." He handed the flashlight to Riley and pulled another from the box. "Each round is fifteen minutes. If you aren't caught by the end of the round, head back on your own. Don't break anything, don't break yourselves, and stay away from the basement. There's snakes down there. Questions?"

"What does he mean there's snakes?" I whispered to Adam.

Adam grinned and took the flashlight extended to him. He handed it to me, and I examined the room.

"All right," Tate said. "Team A, go hide."

Half the room's population scattered like mice. Their shoes echoed against the floor, and the sound of doors opening and closing ricocheted through the building. Adam grabbed the flashlight and turned it off.

"What are you doing?" I asked. My hand brushed his skin as I tried to get it back. "This place is creepy. Turn it on!"

"Watch the hands," he answered. "You might grab something you didn't plan on grabbing." I paused, and his laugh echoed through the room. "You embarrassed, Collins? I've never seen you shut up so quick."

I crossed my arms and turned my back to him. If I pretended to be invisible, maybe I would be.

Something rustled the sleeve of my plaid shirt and made its way up my arm.

"Ah!" I screamed, whacking my shoulder with my hand. "Get off! Get off!"

"Easy, killer," Adam said, his touch becoming more than a light graze. His fingers worked their way down my forearm and reclaimed my hand. "I didn't know where you went. Wanted to make sure you hadn't tried to go it alone."

"I can take care of myself."

"Trust me, I believe you."

He gave my hand a squeeze, and his arm brushed mine. While I was more than confident I could survive this place, Adam eased my nerves. He was comforting in the dark, and he was someone I could sacrifice if I had to run away screaming.

His scent lingered, and his breathing slowed. A few minutes later, the flashlight burned through the night. "Come on," he said, tugging me across the room. "Tate always hides in the same spot."

We found our way to a creepy hall where rusted doors sat shut. "This town needs a bowling alley," I said, darting a glance behind me.

"Shhh."

I glared at the back of Adam's head. "Don't *shhh* me," I replied. "No one died and made you the king of hide-and-go-seek. As a matter of fact, this place belongs to Tate. If anyone should be shushing me, it's—"

Adam turned, catching me off guard as he clasped his hand over my mouth and backed me into the wall.

Well, hello there.

He was a shadow, illuminated only by the beam that reflected off the floor. Strands of his hair brushed my forehead, soft against my skin, while the fabric of his shirt pressed flush against mine. I was pinned against cool metal, but his body was warm.

He was close.

He was too close.

Footsteps echoed down the hall, and he turned, cracking the tension between us as his hand shot out. Tate's aggravated cry bellowed through the dark.

"Dammit, Adam! Why do you always come after me?" He freed himself and huffed. "You're supposed to be my ride or die! Go look for Riley. Leave me in peace."

"You'd sacrifice your girlfriend for your own good?"

"Yes," Tate answered.

Adam shone the light in Tate's face, then motioned down the hall. "You're caught. Do me a favor and find your way back."

"No," Tate argued. "You have to escort your captures or they don't count. Rules are rules."

"I'm busy."

"Do I look like I care?" Tate stumbled and shook his head. "You bring me back, or I wasn't caught."

Adam looked at me, scowling, then sighed and stepped away. "You're an asshole," he told Tate.

"I know."

We walked back to base, but Adam didn't grab my hand again. He was quiet, emotionless. Once we reached base, Tate beelined to the middle of the room.

"Round's up," he said. "Tell anyone still out, they're safe."

"He's a sore loser," Adam said.

"You're a dick," Tate replied. He waited until everyone was back at base, then addressed our team. "You have fifteen minutes to hide." His brown eyes focused on Adam. "And you'd better run. I'm coming for you."

"Good luck."

All flashlights were switched off, and Adam pulled me through the room in the dark. He was quick around objects and people, but I didn't know the space like he did. I knocked into something with an edge and clutched my leg.

"Ouch," I hissed. "That was my femur!"

"Hush or you can't hide with me" was his sympathetic reply.

We stepped into the hall where Tate was caught, and I turned on the flashlight. My eyes searched for the space where Adam and I had stood. It was a dangerous moment and one I hadn't anticipated, but that didn't lessen my nerves. It didn't change that I was attracted to him more than I wanted to be, and it didn't keep me from thinking about what would've happened had Tate hidden somewhere else.

"Come on," Adam said.

He hurried across the concrete, and we ducked into a room with a massive steel door. Something sticky clung to my face, and I backtracked as a fleet of spiders came into view. They were my biggest fear, and we'd stepped into their den.

"It's on me!" I screamed.

My pulse raced, and my screams morphed into panicked breaths that hung in my throat. The world spun as spiders crawled along their webs, curling me in a cocoon of fear that wanted to devour me whole. My head was spinning, but I couldn't move. I couldn't do anything but stare at the ceiling and watch spiders crawl above my head. I was frozen with no way out.

"Claire?"

Adam's voice was distant, only a murmur compared with the beating of my heart.

"Claire?" he repeated.

An arm wrapped around my shoulder and forced me from my spot. Pulled from my state of terror, I screamed again.

"Hold on," Adam said, hurrying through the room.

He paused in front of another steel door and pushed it open with his hip. When we crossed the threshold and I was sure we were safe, I barreled over and tried to control my breathing. Adam stopped beside me.

"I didn't realize you were afraid of spiders."

"Surprise," I choked out.

I surveyed the room, breathing in the thick smell of must as I tried to calm myself. Large objects were everywhere, separated by boxes and covered in dust. One of those objects was a boat like the one we'd used at the lake. Adam walked to it, his footsteps level with his voice.

"This is our hiding spot," he said. "You'll get inside, and I'll stay on the ground. If someone comes in, I'll distract them so you can stay hidden."

I shook my head. "Under no circumstances will I be alone in this building. If I'm getting in the boat, you're getting in the boat. Take it or leave it."

"It's better if I stay on the ground," he said.

"Take it or leave it," I repeated.

He sighed and grabbed my waist, hoisting me upward. I scanned for spiderwebs before my hands wrapped around the metal siding. Adam followed quickly behind.

"Lie down," he said. "They'll see us if you're sitting up."

"Quit being demanding."

"You ordered me up here. You're the one who's demanding."

I did what he asked while he walked to the back of the boat. A tarp was slung across one of the seats, covered with boxes and discarded toys. He tried to retrieve it, but junk fell to the ground and clanged against the concrete.

"Shit," he hissed.

"It's a sign. Leave it alone."

"We'll get caught," he argued. "We need a backup plan, in case they decide to check here."

"That tarp isn't touching me, so you might as well leave it where you found it."

Stone-faced, he stared at me. I mirrored the look.

"Fine," he said, releasing the tarp and returning to the bow, "but you're the worst hiding partner ever. You're scared of spiders, you talk too loud, and you refuse to do anything I ask."

"Then maybe you should've hidden with another girl," I replied. "Word has it you've hooked up with at least one person at this party. She's probably more tolerant than me."

Adam's eyes widened, and I cursed myself up and down for my lack of a filter. This was the slippery slope I'd tried to avoid.

"Which girl are you talking about?" he asked.

"How many girls have there been?"

Metal creaked from the other room, and footsteps followed the noise. I dropped to the bottom of the boat, and Adam dropped beside me, his body flush with my back as I begged the universe to send them away.

"Someone's been in here," a guy said.

"How can you tell?" a girl replied.

"They knocked over a bunch of junk."

Adam's breath grew staggered behind me, so I nudged him with my elbow to get him to hush. He squeezed my side in response.

"You check there," the girl instructed. "I'll look here."

Flashlight beams ricocheted off the room's metal siding, and created eerie shadows as they searched the room. They stayed for what felt like an eternity, but eventually the beams began to fade.

Once the shadows were gone, Adam poked me in the side and leaned closer. His stubble brushed my cheek as he whispered, "We need to reach base before they get back. Ready to go?"

"Go?" I murmured.

He didn't answer. He sat up, peered over the boat, and signaled for me to move. He was first over the side, landing on the floor with the smallest squeak of rubber hitting concrete.

"There he is!" a girl yelled in the dark.

Footsteps quickened, and I flattened against the boat's floor as Adam ran from the seekers. Within seconds, a metal door slammed and the room fell quiet.

I lay there in the dark, waiting for Adam to come back. When I heard nothing but small scurries and mouse squeaks, I decided that wouldn't be anytime soon.

My hand found the boat's siding, and I stumbled over the edge. When I reached the floor, I tried to find an exit. There was no way I'd go back through the spider den, so I hoped for another route out.

I was halfway through my search when a hand wrapped around my bicep and yanked me backward. I swung a fist. I missed, so I swung again.

"Stop!" Adam yelled. "It's me. Geez." A flashlight flickered between us, and he shot me narrowed eyes. "We need to work on you having a reaction other than punching."

"Why are you here?" I replied, dropping my hand. "You're supposed to be at base."

"You told me not to leave you, so I came back. I didn't think you'd leave the boat." He rubbed the shoulder where my hand made contact, then shined the flashlight on a set of double doors at the back of the room. "That's the other way out," he said. "We could go through the first room, but I don't think you would."

"The one with spiders? No."

He nodded and was silent as he unhitched the door. When we got outside, he was still quiet, but it was different from before. His jaw was clenched, his posture rigid, and he kept his eyes anywhere but on me. Something was wrong.

He relatched the door and started to walk away. He got a good ten feet from me before I decided I was done.

"What's wrong with you?" I asked, following him.

"None of your business."

"You mad we got found?"

"No."

"Oh, so your attitude is something you come by naturally?"

"You know what?" he answered, spinning. "*You're* my problem. You and your constant pissing me off."

"What did I do this time?" I asked, stopping in my tracks. "Because it's always something. There's never a happy medium. You're always pissed off about something."

"I'm not always pissed off," he answered. "Am I now? Yeah. I'm really pissed. I'm mad about what you said in the boat."

I rolled my eyes, knowing already where this was headed. "Was I wrong?" I asked, crossing my arms.

"No," he replied. "It was probably the truth."

"Then what's the issue?"

"You throwing it in my face." He shook his head, glaring at me. "Let me be clear, Collins. Who I have and haven't hooked up with has nothing to do with you. It happened, and I own it, but just because someone ran their mouth doesn't mean you have permission to judge me. You don't have that right. You don't even know me."

"I wasn't judging you," I said, "and you're right, I don't know you. I don't know anything but your reputation. Which, I've heard, is spot-on. Congrats!"

"What is that?!" he asked, glaring.

"It's me congratulating you," I answered.

"It's you making passive-aggressive remarks you know are going to make me mad."

"If you knew, why did you ask?"

He moved toward me, his lips pulled into a thin line. "You're the most irritating person I've ever met! It's like you need validation on who I want to be around. If that's what this is, okay.

Here's your validation. I like you, Claire. You're a pain in my ass, but I like you anyway. It makes no sense, but it is what it is."

"You have a really crappy way of showing it," I answered.

"Because I don't want to," he said. "We agreed to keep it simple, and we agreed for a reason. That didn't mean I didn't like you. It didn't mean I was interested in someone else. It was my attempt to keep this from getting complicated, but I can't do that if we aren't on the same page." He raked a hand through his messy hair, his gaze unwavering. "You screw with my head, Claire. I'm supposed to be focused on a million other things, but I can't do that because you're always around pushing my buttons and pissing me off."

"That's how I am. Sorry, but I'm not changing."

"I don't want you to change. That's the problem." He was in front of me now, staring at me eye to eye with such confliction that I could feel it, too.

"And what am I supposed to do with that?" I asked.

"There's nothing you can do," he answered. "You're witty and sarcastic and beautiful, and you don't put up with my crap, and I don't know how to deal with it. That's on me. It isn't your problem."

"It is my problem," I said, "because the last thing I need is another football player breaking my heart. This"—I waved my hand between us—"I've done this. I know what it feels like when it ends. I can't handle it again."

"I'm trying not to break your heart."

"Then don't."

Adam rested his forehead against mine, and we stood like that for a minute—two people torn between want and need.

"Tell me what you want," he whispered, his arms encircling

my waist, "because I feel like I'm stuck between what's right and what isn't."

"What do *you* want?"

"You."

His mouth grazed mine, and I paused. We stood at a crossroads, where one wrong thing had the potential to wreck everything, but there was no use denying it now. Not with Adam. Not when I felt the same. I pulled him back and kissed him again.

11

Trips

"Hey, hun. How was Riley's?"

I dropped my bag beside the door and crossed the living room. It was Saturday. My mom was sprawled on the couch with the cooking channel blaring on the screen and a notepad on her lap. The notepad meant she was trying a new recipe. If we were lucky, she'd forget she wrote it down.

"It was fine," I answered, taking a seat in my dad's recliner. "Dad at the field house?"

"Yeah. He and Case left earlier," she said. "Think they left pancakes on the stove, if you're hungry."

"I'm good."

I glanced at the television, but my mom paused it. She tossed the notepad beside the remote, then shifted so she was facing me.

"Spoke to your dad last night," she said, smiling. "I've been trying not to call you until you got home, but we found a solution."

"A solution for what?" I asked, arching a brow.

"The Baker Heights trip," she answered. "We can go in three weeks. We'll make it a girls' trip."

My heart quickened, and I immediately looked at the bracelet wrapped around my wrist. I begged for this trip, paid my dues to get this trip, but I wasn't excited. I should've been excited.

"Thanks," I said, forcing a smile.

"You're welcome."

She relaxed into the cushions and resumed the television. I stayed there with her, absently watching the rest of the cooking show while I tried to convince myself that I was excited. I couldn't do it.

"Mom," I said as she finished jotting the recipe.

"Yeah?"

"Don't get mad, but I don't know if I want to go anymore." Her attention darted upward. "I've been trying to get over the move," I continued, fidgeting with my bracelet, "and I've been trying to get over Seth. I feel like I'm getting to a place where I can do that. I'm moving on. Visiting Baker Heights would be three steps backward, right?"

She sat there a minute, her eyes on me. The last time I got this look was when I told her I wanted go blond. She looked cautious, filled with things she wanted to say but worried about my reaction.

"What?" I asked, grabbing a throw pillow. "You think it would be better if I went?"

"No," she answered. "I think you're making the right choice. Baker Heights is in the past, and you need to keep moving forward, but this doesn't change that I owe you a trip. A deal is a deal, and you've kept your side of the bargain. If you don't want to go, we'll find another option. I think I might already have one."

"Really?"

She nodded and grabbed her phone from the end table. Two seconds later, she had it to her ear. "Mark," she said, addressing my dad.

I stared at her, brow furrowed.

"Think you can get another ticket for that trip?" she continued. I could hear my dad's muffled voice on the other end of the line. I couldn't hear his response, but a slow smile spread across her face. "Great. Yeah, it's for her. No. No. We'll talk about it later. 'Kay. Love you, too."

"So, where am I going?" I asked.

"That's for me to know and you to find out," she replied.

"Mom!"

"That's my name," she answered.

She went back to her shows, and I spent the next two hours trying to drag the info out of her. By the time my dad and Case got home, I'd expended all options and was sulking in the kitchen.

"What's for lunch?" my dad asked. He glanced at my freshly baked pizza rolls and stole one. "Shit!" he exclaimed, spitting it back on the tray. "Those are hot!"

"Mark! Language."

"What I meant was, Oh my heavens, these pizza rolls are

scorching," he said, smiling at my mom. She whacked him on the shoulder with her notepad, and he laughed. "What?" he said. "My language was fine that time."

"You don't have to be a smart-ass about it."

He kissed her on the cheek and maneuvered around the island. One look at dinner prep, and he cringed. "Looks delicious," he lied.

In reality it looked disgusting. She claimed it was sauce for chicken spaghetti. I had my doubts.

"Did you get the goods?" she asked, looking at him.

"Yes. Why? We doing that now?"

"Now, later, either way is fine with me," she replied.

"Adam's here!" Case hollered, grabbing a pizza roll as he stepped into the kitchen. He popped it in his mouth before I could tell him dad had it first. Only Case would eat an already munched-on pizza roll and not even notice. "Hi, Mrs. Collins," Adam said. "Sorry to barge in."

"It's not barging in if I told you to swing by," my dad answered. He headed to the hall. "I'll be right back. Let me grab that stuff."

"Yes, sir."

Adam's eyes flickered to me, and I adjusted my ponytail. Why hadn't I showered instead of nagging my mom all morning?

He stopped beside me and leaned against the counter. "Hi," he said.

"Hi," I replied.

The corners of his mouth tilted upward, and my mom cleared her throat. When I looked at her, she was staring.

"You're more than welcome to stay for dinner," she said,

addressing Adam. "We're having chicken spaghetti. I'd love to have more taste testers."

"Don't," Case hissed. "You'll never make it out alive."

"You haven't even tried it, Case Michael."

"Wow, breaking out the middle name," I said, grinning.

"You want in on this, Claire Elizabeth?"

"Nope. All I want is my pizza rolls." I turned, ignoring the pair as they bickered over my mom's chicken spaghetti.

Adam watched their back and forth, then took the pizza roll I handed him. "I like them. They're funny."

"Try living with them," I said.

My dad reentered the kitchen and hesitated in the doorway. "What happened? What did I miss?" he asked.

"Mom's spaghetti," I replied. "Case made the mistake of voicing all our concerns."

"Right." He nodded and cleared his throat, earning my mom's and brother's attention. When he flashed a folded piece of paper, she straightened her apron and walked to his side.

"What's happening?" Adam asked.

"No idea." I popped a pizza roll in my mouth. When they faced me, I froze. "What did I do?" I asked. "Besides being the perfect child."

"We have something for you," my mom answered. She bounced across the kitchen, grinning as she handed me the folded piece of paper. "It's from your dad and me."

Slowly, I unwrapped it. When my eyes found *Alabama*, my adrenaline rushed. "Is this . . . Are we . . ."

"We're going to Auburn," my dad replied.

Shocked, I looked at the paper again. Joy flowed down my cheeks. "Thank you!" I cried, running across the kitchen for a hug. "Thank you so much! This is . . . I just . . . is this real?" I scanned the paper. My name was there in black and white. It had to be real.

"We fly out in two weeks," my dad said, his arms crossing his chest. "We'll leave on Saturday and return Monday after school, so both of you need to bring your makeup work with you. You can do it on the plane."

"Both of us?" I repeated. I blinked, confused, as my dad handed Adam a paper that matched mine. No. No. No.

"It's a bye week, so I'm meeting with scouts," Adam explained.

My stomach curled.

"It's Auburn this month, the University of Tennessee next month, and—"

"Clemson wants to see you, too," my dad interrupted. "Got the call on my way home from the field house."

Adam smiled. "They're one of the best teams in the country!"

"No kidding. All we need is the University of Alabama to call, and you've got your pick of the litter."

Adam moved closer to my dad. Talk of national championships became their focal point, but I tuned them out. A trip to Auburn meant a lot of time with Adam. I couldn't decide if I was excited or concerned.

"Your dad and I talked about bringing you to visit Auburn in the spring," my mom said, taking a spot beside Case and me. "When he got the call for Adam to talk to the coaches, to tour campus and their facilities, we talked about getting you a ticket, but decided it would be better to go in the spring. We weren't sure we could swing a trip to Baker Heights *and* a trip to Auburn."

"Auburn will always trump Baker Heights," I said, glancing at her. "That's a no-brainer."

"Then I'm glad it worked out this way," she replied. She paused, studying me. "I know you didn't want to move here because of Seth—"

"Mom."

"—and I know how hard the breakup was on you, but I'm proud of you for moving on. There's a guy out there who will love you regardless of the distance. Who knows, he may even be in this room."

I pinched the bridge of my nose, wishing the embarrassment away. This wasn't happening, not with Adam in earshot. Case thought it was hilarious. He cracked up as soon as she stepped away.

"You're just so grown up," he said, grinning.

"Shut up, Case."

He chuckled and leaned over the counter, grabbing another pizza roll. "So, Auburn with Meade?"

I shifted my face from his view. Case was a master at reading through my crap. He'd caught my hesitation and wanted to bug me about it.

He crammed the pizza roll in his mouth, then studied Adam across the room. "Be careful," he said, his voice dropping.

I glanced at him. Something about the way he said it set me on edge.

"What does that mean?" I asked.

Case's expression was neutral, but his eyes flickered from Adam to our parents, calculating.

"Case, what does that mean?" I repeated.

He took another pizza roll and turned so his back was to our parents. Adam was out of sight, covered by Case's graphic tee and towering form. "I'm not saying it's true," he said, "but I know Adam's reputation. He has it for a reason, Claire. Watch out. Okay?"

I nodded, and Case exited the kitchen. Most of the time Case was a moron, but he was usually right when it came to guys. He worried about my relationship with Seth, and it ended just like he said it would, with me heartbroken. I would be an idiot to ignore him and let the same thing happen again.

"Question."

I glanced at Adam as he crossed the kitchen, grinning with the paper tight in his hand.

"How would you feel about a game of Scrabble and some homemade peach cobbler?" he said. "I caught a better look at that spaghetti. Pretty sure it's inedible."

"You're learning quick," I replied. I cocked my head. "But are you sure about the cobbler? I thought you said you didn't share?"

"People change. Even me."

"You sure about that, Meade?"

"Positive."

* * *

"I'm telling you she likes me more than you," I said, noshing on a cookie. "You can deny it all you want, but I'm cooler. These cookies prove it."

"Those were my cookies, and you stole them." Adam pulled his truck down Tate's road, nothing but darkness and stars visible from the windows. "Besides," he said, "it was a test recipe for some guy she met at the VFW dance. She gave you the crappy batch and left the good ones on the stove."

"Someone sounds bitter," I said. I bit into another chocolate chip and sighed. "So, Wanda has a boyfriend?"

"Wanda has someone calling her up," Adam answered. "Wouldn't say they're serious. They've bonded over Scrabble Club, but I think he's faking. The guy probably hates Scrabble. He seems like a domino lover."

"Old people scandals. The horror."

He gave me a look, one somewhere between amusement and annoyance. "Don't make me pull this truck over, Claire Collins. I'm likely to throw you into the Macks' pond. You'll be the town's newest ice statue."

"And I'll die of hypothermia and come back to haunt you."

"Or you'll have to strip and cuddle with me for body warmth," he replied. "It'll be a life or death thing. I'll totally help you out."

"Do you ever think with your upper head?"

"Yes, but it's rare." I shoved him and he pointed a finger at me. "That's called distracting the driver, sweetheart."

"Call me sweetheart one more time and I'll—"

"Kiss me senseless, then blame me for your unprovoked actions?"

"You'd like that too much."

"I definitely wouldn't complain." I rolled my eyes, and he laughed. "Just saying, there's still a good mile between us and Tate's house. We've got time, and I know the back roads. If my truck accidentally gets stuck . . ."

I shook my head. That would be like Adam to know the back roads. He probably used them for all the wrong reasons and would get stuck on purpose.

"You're considering it, aren't you?" he asked.

"Nope," I answered. "I already told Riley we'd be there soon, and I'm not the kind of girl who ditches her friends for a guy. You want my time, you'll have to take a number."

Adam's jaw dropped as he pulled the truck to a stop. "Take a number?" he replied.

"You could be number two?"

"Number two?" he said, taking the keys out of the ignition. "I'm sorry. Number two won't do."

He shut his door and walked around the truck. When he reached my side and opened the door, I caught the mischief in his eyes.

"Adam, don't do anything irrational." He motioned for me to get out of the truck, but I shook my head. It was chilly, and the truck was warm. This didn't seem like the best-thought-out plan.

"Claire, you have to get out of the truck."

"No. I'm perfectly happy right where I am."

"It's my truck. Get out." I gave him the same look my mom gave my dad when he was being an ass. When he continued with "Get out of the truck, *please*," I knew I'd been successful. I needed to use that more often.

Adam grabbed his letter jacket from the back seat and tossed it to me. "You'll want this."

"Why? What are we doing?"

"Don't worry about it," he answered. "Quit asking questions and go with the flow. It's a bit of a walk, but it'll be okay. I promise."

I followed him across the grass. Beneath the full moon, it was easy to spot the abandoned barn on Tate's property. It loomed far in the distance, with small buildings farther behind.

"If I get bit by a snake, I'm going to be mad," I said.

"If you get mad, you'll be stuck in the country by yourself."

He grinned at me over his shoulder and extended his hand. I took it, my fingers linking with his. "You always like this when a guy takes you out?" he asked, looking ahead. "And I mean whiny. Not in a good way."

I extended my boot and caught his ankle. He stumbled in the grass, laughing as he straightened to full height.

"I'm not whiny," I answered, "and no, I'm not always like this. If you'd quit being a jackass, maybe I'd be nicer."

"I'm being a perfect gentleman, Collins. I gave you my jacket. I'm holding your hand. I happen to know most girls like both of those things."

"How many girls did you ask?" I replied.

"More than I should probably admit." I squeezed his hand, and his laugh carried on the breeze. "You know how I am," he said. "It's not like I've tried to keep it a secret. As a matter of fact, I'm the only one whose personal stuff is out there in the open. What about you? When are you planning on sharing your past with me?"

"I don't have a past," I lied.

"Yeah, not buying that for a second."

I pulled my lip between my teeth and tried to figure out where to start. This conversation had to happen eventually, I just didn't expect it this soon. I needed time to prepare. Where did I even start?

"I have one ex," I said, looking at Adam. "And it's complicated."

"I'm sure I can keep up."

"Okay," I answered. "My ex and I dated. We broke up. The end."

"I need more than that, Collins. Nice try."

I groaned and scowled at him. He held my gaze, a smile still present on his face.

"What do you want to know?" I asked, my tone taking on an edge. "It was good, and then it wasn't. We started dating when we were sophomores, and we broke up this summer."

"You don't sound like you're over it."

"I am." Adam shot me a skeptical look, and I shook my head, my cheeks heating despite the cold. "What do you want me to say, Adam?" I asked, stopping. "He broke my heart. He told me he didn't care if my dad took this job. He told me we'd make it work because he loved me. I trusted him. I thought he meant what he said, but he didn't. He lied. He told me everything I wanted to hear, but when the time came to move, he was done. He wanted his freedom." I paused. "He didn't want me."

Ahead, a flashlight beam flickered on. Adam paused, frowning as he turned toward me.

"And it hurt," I said. "I was in love with him, but it didn't matter. It wasn't enough."

"Are you still in love with him?" Adam asked, his face void of expression.

"No," I answered. "I've moved on. I'm happy for the first time in a long time, and you're a big part of that. I care about you. If I didn't, I wouldn't be here."

Adam nodded and pulled me into a warm hug.

"And I don't want to talk about Seth," I said, looking at him.

"His name is Seth?" When I nodded, Adam cupped my cheeks in his hands. "Well, Seth sounds like an asshole anyway," Adam replied. He kissed me as Tate's voice echoed across the pasture, but pulled away before they were close enough to see.

Riley and Tate came to a stop in front of us, Riley smiling as she eyed the letter jacket I wore. "Tate, have you ever seen Adam let a girl wear that jacket?"

"Nope," Tate answered, shaking his head. "I've seen many try, but all have failed."

"Adam's standing right in front of you," Adam replied. He crammed his hands in his pockets and looked around the space. "You bring your clubs?"

"Brought mine and borrowed my dad's," Tate said. "Everything is set up and waiting on us to get there."

"Clubs?" I repeated, looking at Riley for insight.

"Night golf," Riley replied.

"You golf?" I asked Adam.

"Heck yes, I golf. I'm a man of many wonders, Collins. I golf. I play baseball. I do it all."

"We're triple threats," Tate explained. "The best athletes to ever come through Pader."

"And when one of you ends up in the hospital with a concussion, I'll remember you said that," Riley said. "Because it isn't night golf until someone gets pegged in the head. I just hope it isn't Tate."

Distractions

"You don't get back until Sunday?"

"Monday afternoon," I clarified.

I closed the locker, and Riley followed me through the school's back doors. On Fridays, cheerleaders wore their uniforms to school. The bells on her shoes clinked with each step, drawing attention as we crossed the parking lot.

"And is this only a football thing, or do the pair of you plan on hanging out alone?" she asked. I gave her the side-eye, and she grinned. "Just wondering," she said. "Things haven't been the same since the two of you disappeared during hide-and-go-seek. You seemed pretty friendly the other night."

"Nothing's changed," I said. I stopped at my car and tossed my backpack in the trunk. When I turned, Riley was wide eyed.

"Do you seriously think I haven't noticed you two sneaking time away?" she asked.

"What time?"

"Um, lunch."

My cheeks heated. Okay. Fair enough. "I had to print out more scholarship applications," I said. "Case broke the printer at home, and I wanted to work on them during the plane ride tomorrow."

"Right, because printing out applications is the same as sneaking out here and chatting in Adam's truck," she said. I paused and darted a glance around the parking lot. "The sun's more likely to crash into the earth than Adam is to give up half a cheeseburger. If you don't want people to know what's going on, be more careful. That piece of info was courtesy of a member of the cheer squad who asked me if you two were dating."

"Someone asked you about us?"

She nodded.

I cringed and continued walking. Adam and I weren't official, but we were kind of committed. I don't know. It was a big mess that needed to be sorted sooner rather than later. Adding nosy people to the mix wouldn't help.

"I'd bet money you come back as a couple," Riley said. "Watch."

"Who's a couple?" Tate asked, meeting us as we passed through senior parking. He wore his game day attire and a duffel bag on his shoulder.

"Her and Adam," Riley told him.

Tate glanced at me and shrugged. "Not getting involved. Adam's my bro, but his personal life is his thing."

"What a great way of thinking," I remarked.

Riley deflated. "You're supposed to be on my side, Tate."

"I *am* on your side." He kissed her cheek and pivoted. "Just because I don't meddle doesn't mean you can't. One of us has to get the info."

He waved good-bye and jogged to the field house. Guys were already filing onto the bus. Their conversations drifted through open bus windows into the cool afternoon. I didn't catch Adam's voice, but that didn't mean he wasn't on board.

"Just know I support you as a pair," Riley said, "and if he's a jerk to you in any way, call me. I'll take a pair of fingernail clippers to his hair. He likes his hair. It's the quickest way to inflict pain."

"Noted."

I waved at her and walked to the bus.

Adam sat in the seat behind the driver. His mouth was twisted as he quietly scanned a page of *x*'s and *o*'s.

"This seat taken?" I asked, stopping beside him.

"I'm actually waiting on the water girl," he said. "Pretty sure she stood me up, but you're a good alternative." I arched a brow, and he shifted to let me in. "Okay fine, but don't tell her I let you sit with me. Her dad's the coach."

"Yikes. Heard you run sprints if you piss him off."

"Crap. Maybe you should find another seat."

I elbowed him in the side, and he chuckled, returning to the playbook. A few minutes later, my dad boarded, and the bus pulled away from the school.

Through the window, trees passed in blurs of green and gold. The leaves had changed within the last week, carrying the onset of autumn and cooler weather.

I relaxed into the seat and leaned against the window. Acoustic music played through my earbuds, drowning all other noise until it was halted by the *ping* of a text message.

I glanced at the screen, annoyed as I read the text.

Seth: What are you doing?

I deleted the text.

Seth: We aren't talking anymore?

Adam shifted beside me, his arm warm through his button-down. He tucked the playbook into my dad's briefcase, and I removed my earbuds. My phone buzzed, but I put it under my leg to muffle the sound.

"You excited about tomorrow?" he asked, poking my Auburn bracelet.

"Yeah. Excited, but nervous."

"I get it," he answered. "College prospects are awesome, and I'm glad I have them, but it'll be weird moving out of my grandma's house. Been with her since I was twelve. Don't know how she'll function without me."

"Think you'll go as far as Alabama?" I asked. "Or leaning toward staying closer to home?"

"Anything is possible, Collins."

"Sounds like your way of avoiding an answer."

"Ask me after we visit Auburn," he said, chuckling.

"Okay. I will."

* * *

"I'm so tired," Adam groaned.

"Same."

I smudged mascara from beneath my eyes and stared at my dad. He was just as exhausted as everyone else, but it was his fault. Who schedules a flight at six a.m. on a Saturday?

"Didn't work," he said, staring at the tickets as he approached us. "Tried to get our seats switched so we're all beside each other, but the plane is full. Right now, we have two seats at the front and one in the middle of the plane. If you want, the pair of you can take the seats at the front."

"I want the window seat," I said, looking at Adam.

"That's fine. I need an aisle seat anyway. If not, I'll be stiff when we get there."

"Great," my dad said, handing us tickets before heading to security.

"Have I told you how awesome your dad is?" Adam asked, watching him as he left. "Because he's seriously one of the coolest people I've ever met."

"Remember that when he starts singing Broadway songs," I replied. "Nothing on this planet can save you from a Mark Collins cover."

Charlotte International was crowded. I expected a handful of people, but the security line was already twenty deep. I got in line in front of Adam and waited my turn. When I was up, I placed my polka-dot carry-on on the conveyor, slid off my ankle boots, and tossed my jewelry into a plastic bin beside them. Two seconds later, I was through to the other side.

Adam was next, but the metal detector beeped on his first step through.

"You broke it," I said. "Way to go."

He frowned at me and took a step back, waiting for permission before he tried to pass through again. When he set off the metal detector a second time, one of the TSA agents came over. Adam stared at him, brow furrowed.

"Any metal objects?" the agent said.

"No, sir," Adam replied. "I had hand surgery when I was younger. There's a permanent set of screws in my left hand and a rod in my wrist, but I didn't think it would set off the detector."

"Medical ID card?" the guy questioned.

"No, sir."

"Ever flown before?"

"No, sir."

"If you're flying, you need to get one."

The agent escorted Adam to another area as my dad passed through the detector. "Meade's having a hard time," he said, pulling his shoes from the conveyor. "Can you wait here for him? I want to check the gate and make sure our plane isn't delayed."

"Yeah. We'll meet you at the gate."

I put my ring on, slid the bracelet over my wrist, and put on my boots. When Adam finally made it through, he grabbed his stuff and took a seat beside me.

"Didn't know you had hand surgery when you were younger," I said. "Was it football related?"

"It's a long story," he replied. He tied his shoes, stood, and lifted his shirt to put his belt on. The scar I saw at the lake showed above his waistband, long and jagged against tanned skin. "Where's your dad?" he asked.

"He went to check the flight status."

Adam nodded and grabbed my duffel from the floor. Once

both of our bags were slung over his shoulder, he extended his hand. "I need coffee," he said. "You up for some?"

"Absolutely."

We located the closest Starbucks and sipped it while we waited to board.

"Riley talk to you about the bet?" he asked, glancing at me over his cup.

I cringed. "Please tell me she didn't bring that up."

"She did," he said. "There's about fifty bucks involved. Twenty from her, betting we'll get together, twenty from Tate betting we won't, and ten from me saying we will but it won't last."

"Lovely," I answered, shaking my head.

"My thoughts are we get together, then break up, so I win," Adam explained. "We can take the money and split it. What do you say?"

"That's brilliant!" I replied.

He chuckled and finished his coffee, flagging my dad over as he returned to the gate.

Fifteen minutes later, we were passing through an enclosed tunnel. When we reached our seats, the plane was already half full. Adam volunteered to put the bags in the overhead compartment.

"Push harder," I said, feigning a smile at the grumpy old people waiting to get by. Adam glared at me over his shoulder. "Please."

"You want to do it?" he replied.

He shifted his body so he was more in the seat. It allowed the older people room to get by. They grumbled at him as they passed through the little space available.

"Blame this one," he said. "She had to pack thirty pairs of

shoes. I told her she only needed one pair, but she's so stubborn and refuses to listen to—"

My elbow connected with his abs, and he sucked in a breath.

"Oops," I said.

"You'll be saying oops when I tell the flight attendant you're being violent," Adam replied. He shifted back into the aisle and tried the bag again. With one hard push, he crammed it into the tiny space. "Victory!" he exclaimed, throwing his hands in the air.

He dropped into the seat beside me. With people still filing through the plane's open doors, he had no choice but to keep his long legs between our seat and the one in front of us. His knees were almost to his chest.

"Need more room?" I said, smiling.

"That's an understatement."

He pulled his phone from his pocket as Wanda's name lit up the screen. Rather than reading the text over his shoulder, I looked out the window.

Outside, darkness was starting to give way to the morning. Hues of orange and gold streaked across the horizon, fading away the stars. I was still focused on the sunrise when the plane started to pull away from the gate. Adam leaned over my lap, his voice a distraction from the view outside.

"This is where they come out, right?" he asked.

I blinked at him, confused.

"The air mask things," he said. "Do they drop from here? Also, do they automatically help you breathe or is there more?" The plane stopped, and his attention darted to the window. "Why did we stop? Is there something wrong?"

"There's a flight in front of us that hasn't left yet," I answered. "We have to wait our turn."

"Right. I knew that."

"Sure you did." I surveyed him and saw the tension in his jaw and the stiffness in his demeanor. "Forgot to mention this was your first time flying? Scared?"

"Ha. You wish."

He leaned across me, smelling of body wash and laundry detergent. He was a blanket of warmth, and his forearms rested against the top of my thighs as his eyes swept the sky.

His breathing grew rapid as the plane began to move again, readying for takeoff.

"How fast is this going to go?" he whispered. "Is it zero to sixty or is it a slow increase?"

The plane increased its speed and raced down the runway. Adam's eyes shut as he released a shaky exhale.

"I can't do this," he muttered. "I can't do this."

"Thought you said you weren't scared."

"I lied."

His chest rose and fell in rapid succession, and his grip was so tight on the armrest I was afraid it would crack.

I rested my hand against the top of his knuckles. "Give me your hand," I said. "We'll be in the air in a matter of seconds. Outside of the landing, takeoff is the hardest part." His fingers wrapped around the top of my hand, shaking and sweaty against my skin. "Good. Now ask me a question. It can be whatever you want, just nothing super personal."

"W-why?" he stammered.

"Just do it."

The plane shook a little, and Adam exhaled sharply. "Why do you want to go to Auburn?" he asked. "Is there a reason, or is it just a school you picked?"

I hesitated. There was more than one answer to that question. "My grandpa was a fan," I said after a moment. "He introduced me to Auburn when I was eight. I've wanted to go ever since."

"Did he graduate from there?"

"No. He grew up outside Tuscaloosa and was raised on Alabama. If he would've gone anywhere, it probably would've been there."

"Then why did he like Auburn?"

I shrugged. "During his rebellious phase, he decided to switch football allegiance to their biggest rival—Auburn."

"He became an Auburn fan just to irritate his family?" When I nodded, Adam chuckled. "Sounds like a pretty headstrong guy."

"He was."

The rubber Auburn bracelet sat flush against my skin. The second reason, while less significant, hung over my head like a ton of bricks. I considered telling Adam, but the flight attendant announced use of all approved electronic devices. He quickly pulled a set of earbuds from his pocket, and hit the music app.

"You working on scholarship stuff?" he asked.

"Yeah."

He started his music, and I reached for my tote. There was more to the Auburn story, but I'd lost the opportunity to come clean. I'd let the moment slip away, knowing the truth would eat away at me.

I glanced at Adam again, and my stomach knotted. Maybe it

was easier this way. If we didn't work, I'd never have to tell him at all.

"Claire?"

"Yeah?" I asked, meeting his eyes.

"Thanks for distracting me."

"Anytime."

Trouble

Auburn was beautiful. Covered with aged red-brick buildings, lush green lawns, and students hanging out, the campus was everything I hoped it would be and more.

With the semester in full swing, the Student Center buzzed with people. The scent of coffee filled the air and mixed with the greasy aroma of pizza. Through large windows, warm sunshine heated my skin. I felt at home, sipping Starbucks through a green straw while my newest Auburn additions sat beside me on the floor.

Auburn was my future. All I had to do was graduate, and I'd be here for good.

"You look like you could use some company." My cheeks warmed as I spotted Adam strolling toward me. "Unless another guy called this seat," he said. "In which case, tell him I said to eff off."

He plopped into the seat beside me and rested his arm behind my shoulder.

"Why aren't you in meetings?" I asked, taking a sip of coffee. "Thought you two were busy all day."

"We are," he answered, "but I wanted to see you."

"My bullshit meter is firing on all cylinders," I replied. "Why are you really here?"

"Because I wanted food, and there's a Chick-fil-A on this floor," he answered.

"That excuse I believe." I poked the Auburn lanyard around his neck. It blended with his blue polo. "You two tour the stadium?" I asked. "Get a behind-the-scenes look at Tiger football?"

"We did."

"And?"

He shrugged. "It's nice, but I'm still checking out my other options. Clemson and Alabama are on the radar, too."

My eyes darted around the room. "Don't say that word around here," I whispered. "They'll throw you out before you even get in."

"Which word? Alabama?" I nudged him in the side, and he laughed. "You might like it here, but Auburn doesn't seem like the right fit for me. I'm free to say *Alabama* all I'd like."

My brow furrowed at his dismissal of Auburn. "What's wrong with Auburn?" I asked. "This is a nice school."

"It's a great school," he agreed.

"Then what's the problem?" I replied.

"Nothing, but I still have other football programs I need to check out. I'm keeping my options open." He leaned forward and pulled something from the back of his waistband. I sipped my coffee, quiet as he scanned my face. "You look pissed," he said, fidgeting with a piece of paper. "What did I do and how do I fix it?"

"I'm not pissed," I said. "I'm annoyed."

"Why?"

"No school compares to Auburn," I answered.

"That's your opinion. I have mine."

"Your opinion is wrong," I said, forcing a smile. "I mean that in the nicest way possible."

"Really?" Adam cocked his head to the side, his jaw tight. "Just because I disagree with you doesn't mean I'm wrong. Quit trying to force Auburn on me."

"I'm not."

"Yes, you are." He frowned, his gaze unwavering. "Why do you care about my opinion anyway? You're coming here regardless."

"I care because of this," I answered, waving my hand between us.

Adam paused and his mouth pursed. He looked like he was fighting an answer. His hesitation made me want it more.

"Say it," I said. "Whatever's floating around in your head, just say it."

"This is why I wanted to keep it simple," he said.

He stood and handed me the piece of paper, but I was stuck on his words.

"We passed simple a long time ago," I answered, standing as well.

"I'm not doing this with you," he said, raking a hand through his hair. "I have other football things to do today, and I need to be thinking about the game. Not you."

"Then leave."

He left the Student Center, and I sat back down and finished my coffee, seething as my fingers ran over the neon piece of paper. He had some nerve. We agreed on simple, but we were past that. Why was this an issue now?

Confused, I rubbed my temples. What should've been a good time exploring campus turned into an afternoon concentrated on Adam Meade. My trip to Auburn had somehow turned into a drama-filled nightmare.

The sun was going down when I met him and my dad on the concourse. Adam trailed behind us, his eyes on his phone. I ignored him. If he wouldn't look at me, I wouldn't talk to him.

The ride to the hotel was so tense that even my dad seemed to feel it. He glanced at me across the console, looked at Adam in the rearview mirror, then back at me.

"You two headed to dinner before your thing?" he asked.

I arched a brow. "What thing?"

"The neon run," Adam said quietly from the back seat.

I turned and stared at him while my dad pulled the car into the hotel parking lot.

"Okay," my dad answered. "Great conversation." He opened his door and stepped into the cool afternoon, leaving Adam and me alone.

"What neon run?" I asked as soon as the door shut.

"The one I gave you the flyer for," Adam replied.

I fished around my tote for the paper. I hadn't looked at it after our talk at the Student Center. I scanned the information while Adam slid out of the car.

"A 5K?!" I shook my head and followed Adam, matching his pace as he crossed rows of cars. "You want me to run a 5K?!" I said. "Uh-uh. The last time I ran for distance was in the eighth grade. You can clock me on a calendar!"

"There's a party, too," Adam answered, his eyes ahead. "I wanted to take you, before you got pissed at me for no reason."

"I had a reason," I said, lowering my voice.

"Really? Please enlighten me because I obviously missed it."

"You started this," I replied. "*You* kissed *me*, remember? You're the one who asked me to go to your grandma's house. You're the one who invited me to Tate's. You always call me first. You always do everything first. You initiated all of this, and I'm sorry, but I took that to mean you like me. That might have been a mistake on my part, but don't tell me to keep it simple when you're the one who made it complicated. If you don't want me, don't lead me on."

"I don't know what I want."

"Then you need to figure it out because I'm not going to wait around for you."

My strides were long against the asphalt, purposeful and determined. It hurt me to say that to him, to see the shock settle on his face, but I was tired of being the fragile girl who waited on a guy. Maybe I could credit that to Auburn, or maybe Claire Collins was becoming herself again. Either way, I wasn't a pushover. The sooner Adam realized that, the better.

* * *

A documentary played on the television, drowning my dad's snores as he slept on the bed across from me. The room smelled of freshly laundered sheets, but I munched on Cheetos, which severely muddled their cotton scent.

My phone was loud as it rattled against the nightstand.

Adam: Be ready in five

The breath caught in my chest. I hadn't expected to hear from him until the next morning. Even then, I expected him to be more frigid than Antarctica.

Claire: Be ready for what?
Adam: The run

I stood, my stomach churning as I walked to the bathroom and caught a look at myself in the mirror. From my tired blue eyes and wayward ponytail to my newly purchased Auburn sweatpants, I looked like a hot mess.

My feet crossed the carpet, and I grabbed my phone before tugging my duffel off the floor.

Claire: Ten minutes
Adam: Seven

I traded my sweatpants for a pair of shorts, tossed on a Pader High football tee, and tugged on my socks. I was reaching for a hairbrush when a fist rapped against the room's heavy door.

My dad's snore broke off as he raised himself up on his forearm. "Yeah, I'm awake," he muttered.

"It's only Adam," I replied.

"Oh. Never mind."

He rolled onto his stomach, and I checked the peephole to make sure I was right. Adam stood on the other side, dressed in a gray T-shirt and black athletic shorts. He sighed, glanced at the door again, then covered the peephole with his palm.

"Quit staring at me and get out here," he said through the door.

"My dad's sleeping," I answered, tugging it open. "Be patient."

"I am being patient. You're the one who's two minutes late." I scowled and he rolled his eyes. "The thing starts after sundown, and it's already six. I don't want to miss it."

"Then you should've given me more than seven minutes to get ready," I answered.

"You're already gorgeous. Didn't think it would take you much time."

I paused, ignoring the fluttering of butterflies that ran through me. This was exactly my point. Adam tossed out stupid flattering comments but expected me to keep things simple. He was setting me up for failure.

"Let me get my shoes on," I said.

"Okay. Don't forget to grab the car keys. I already asked your dad."

I nodded and shut the door in his face. Two minutes later, I wrote my dad a brief note to tell him we'd left, then grabbed the rental car keys. Adam leaned against the wall, his phone to his ear. He extended his hand for the keys and led the way through the hotel.

"So, it went okay?" he said into his cell phone, unlocking the car as we crossed the parking lot.

I glanced at his profile, caught sight of the frown on his face, and knew something was up.

"Just let me know," he said, pulling open my door. "I can take you if I need to."

I tried not to eavesdrop, but there was no way not to. When he ended the call with *I love you*, I glanced at him.

"Wanda?"

"Yep."

"Everything okay?"

He looked at me, his eyes hard. "Not really," he answered, "but I want to have a good night with you. Let's have fun tonight and worry about everything else tomorrow. Deal?"

I nodded.

Neon for a Cause was held on the massive lawn beside the Student Center. We passed neon arches, music blaring around us as we continued across the grass through flocks of people. Everywhere I looked, people were decked in neon running gear with glow-in-the dark accessories. They buzzed with excitement, making me excited, too.

Adam grabbed my hand as we walked toward the registration desk. A staff member sat behind it. Her face was painted so that it glowed beneath the black-lighted, inflatable entrance.

"There's neon paint each mile," she said to the registrants. "You can pick up your shirts over there. Here's your wristbands. You need these to access the after-party." She looped a set of neon yellow bracelets around the students' wrists, then looked at us. "Registration forms are over there."

"Great. Thanks."

Adam grabbed a set of clipboards and handed me one. My stomach knotted at the idea of running in front of people, but I filled it out anyway. Once the woman had both clipboards, she placed the forms in a folder and started to explain the race instructions. I tuned her out. I needed to find the willpower to run this race when my nerves screamed at me to run away.

"Hey," Adam said, tilting his face into view. "You need your bracelet."

"Oh. Right."

I blinked and apologized to the woman. She slid a yellow bracelet beside my blue Auburn one already wrapped around my wrist. We passed the shirt table, not wanting to keep up with extra clothing, and found the starting line. People hovered there, consuming the space and crowding me in.

START was written on two inflatable structures that glowed white. I looked at them, glanced at the crowd again, and shook my head.

"I need to leave," I said, backing away.

"Claire?" Adam caught me, and I shook my head as his hand loosely wrapped around my forearm. "What's up? What did I do?"

"You didn't do anything," I answered, "but I can't do this race."

"Can't or won't?"

"Both." I swallowed, shifting the weight on my feet as I started, "I should've said something in the car, but I thought I could handle it. I can't. Running in front of people makes me anxious. I had a bad experience when I was younger, got lapped in front of a stadium of people, and it stuck with me. Besides, I don't even remember the last time I hit the track. I'd keel over before we made it past the first mile. You'd have to drag my life-less corpse across the finish line, and I don't think that's the kind of photo finish you'd want." I blew out a shaky breath, and his face softened. "I'm sorry. I thought I could do this, but I can't. You're more than welcome to run. I'll wait for you here."

"We'll skip it," Adam replied. "I'm only here for the after-party."

"You don't have to do that."

"I know. I want to." He studied a tent in the distance and held up a finger. "Think you can wait here for a second? I have an idea."

Confused, I followed his gaze. "What idea?"

"It's a surprise." He walked backward toward the tent. "Stay here for a minute. Try not to flirt with too many guys."

"I'll try," I said, smiling.

I glanced at the massive silhouette of Jordan-Hare Stadium, then at the series of booths that lined the lawn beneath it. Tents were everywhere, with different sororities and fraternities passing out water or food or both. There was a bounce house on one side of the race, a foam pit on the other, and in the distance, a huge inflatable pool.

Something wet hit my back. I froze but my pulse quickened as neon saturated my black shirt and cascaded down my bare legs, leaving trails of paint in its wake.

"You look like someone threw paint on you," Adam said. His mouth was beside my ear, and the hair on the back of my neck raised as more paint fell down my spine. "Tell me, who would go around spilling perfectly good paint?"

I turned and Adam stood there, a bucket of paint in one hand and illuminated fingers on the other.

"Did you really do that?" I asked, gawking at him as his smile glowed beneath the lights.

"Possibly."

I hesitated. Then, before my face gave me away, I ran at him.

"I lied!" Adam cried, trying to run as paint sloshed everywhere. "It was that guy! He did it!"

"Come back and face me like a man!" I yelled.

Adam ran behind a tree and sat the bucket down. He raised his hands. "Okay," he said. "Before we continue, please realize this bucket cost me twenty bucks. We're wasting it."

"You threw paint on me!"

I glared, and he smiled again. "You're like a star," he explained, "except you're smaller and less gaseous. Kind of. Either way, I want to call a truce."

"You want to call a truce?" I repeated. He nodded and I walked to him, my hands out. "Fine. Truce."

We shook hands before he tilted mine upward and linked it with his. "It's so much easier when I don't have to convince you," he said. "Why can't you be this agreeable all the time? It's nice. I like it."

"Because ninety percent of the time you're an asshole," I replied. "It's your default reaction for everything."

"You think you know me so well, don't you?"

"A little." I shrugged. "I also happen to know you love surprises. Not the big ones. The small ones that come without warning."

I dipped my free hand in the paint and smeared it across the planes of his face. His eyes widened, light green beneath vibrant neon.

"See," I said. "You look happy already."

His tongue ran across his teeth as he released my hand. He touched the paint on his face, and after one look at the neon on his fingers, he stared at me again. "Claire."

"What?"

"You'd better run."

I took off, and Adam sprinted after me, forgetting the twenty-dollar bucket of paint as he caught me by the waist and tossed me over his shoulder.

"You think you're real funny, Collins," he said, laughing as he navigated the crowd, "but it's time you got a real lesson on exactly who you're dealing with."

"Let me down!"

"No."

Music pounded louder as we passed tents, the foam pit, and the bounce house. The smell of chlorine invaded my senses as we entered an area labeled POOL OF WONDERS. He wouldn't. Surely, he wouldn't.

"Adam, don't you dare!"

"Don't I dare what?" He paid the guy at the entrance and carried me to a set of cubbies positioned near the front.

"Adam!" I repeated, watching over his shoulder as he slid off his shoes, then grabbed mine. "Think about this for a second."

"I did. I thought about it for one second."

He tossed his phone in the cubby behind our shoes and dug into my pocket for mine. That earned him a hard pinch to his hip. "Sorry," he said, grinning. "I wasn't copping a feel. I was saving your phone from death by water."

He turned and descended metal steps. Panic set in.

"You're being irrational," I said.

"I'm getting payback," he answered. "Sounds pretty rational to me." I gripped the railing, but his hand pried mine away. "Hold your breath."

"Adam—"

I was cut off, submerged into a pool of neon liquid. Adam Meade, asshole extraordinaire, had thrown me in a pool!

He was a dead man.

I pushed myself to the surface and rubbed water from my eyes. Adam's arm encircled my waist from behind, pulling me flush against his chest.

"Glad to know you can swim," he said, stubble grazing my neck.

When I turned, dark brown hair was plastered to his forehead. Neon droplets fell from the end, leaving streaks of paint down his face. I looped my arms around his neck, while his hands splayed across my lower back.

"Did you really do that?" I asked, his long legs stretching beneath me. When he nodded, I dunked him under. "Just making sure."

I swam for the side, hoping I could get myself out of the pool before he caught me. The effort was in vain. Adam swam like a fish and latched on to my leg as soon as my hand touched the ladder.

"You had to get me back," he said, dragging me underneath.

I held my breath and pushed myself upward. As soon as I hit the surface, he pulled me to him. He smiled through streaks of paint, while his eyes swept my face.

"You think you're real funny," I said.

"I think I'm a little funny," he replied. One of his hands released me and pushed a strand of hair behind my ear. "I also think I'm brilliant and a hell of a catch."

"And arrogant."

"And you like me anyway."

"I do."

His gaze held an intensity that pierced my caution and brought my resolve bubbling to the surface. His hand slid from my exposed lower back to midway up my spine. I shivered at his touch, and goose bumps sprawled across my skin.

"You shouldn't," he said, his voice soft. "I know you were mad at me earlier, but I still had a point. Neither of us knows where we'll be at the end of the year. Why would we put ourselves in a situation we can't win?"

"Because sometimes it's easier to go with it," I answered. "It's scary, believe me, I know, but it's better than pretending we're just friends. We're more than friends, Adam."

"I know that, but it doesn't mean it's okay. I don't want to be the guy who breaks your heart. Don't make me be that guy, Claire."

"You make your own choices," I answered. "If you don't want to break my heart, you won't. The choice is yours, but I'm not begging you for a relationship. I'm not going to hope you'll come around and realize what you're missing. I deserve better than that. You know I deserve better than that, and I refuse to be an option if you're—"

His lips grazed mine, barely making contact.

"—if you're not sure what you want," I whispered.

I stared at him, my eyes meeting his. Adam pushed my buttons every day. He tested me, confused me, and was everything I wanted but everything I knew to avoid. I understood his hesitation, better than he knew, but we were beyond the point of simple. We couldn't switch back to friends, just like that.

My hands rested at the base of his neck, and I pulled him to me, taking his bottom lip between my teeth and tugging it gently. "If you're going to kiss me," I said, "do it like you mean it or don't do it at all."

His lips spread into a slow smile. "You sure about that, Collins?"

"I'm sure."

He wedged me against the pool's wall before his mouth slanted over mine. Calloused fingers found my cheeks, and Adam's body pushed against me, hot and damp against my own soaked clothes. He was a wall of muscle, strong and large enough to block out the rest of the world. My hand slid over his shoulder blade and down his spine, fingernails digging into the wet fabric as he deepened the kiss.

Someone cleared a throat above us, and Adam peeled himself away. My cheeks burned with embarrassment as the event moderator scowled and motioned for us to get out of the pool.

I pulled myself over the pool's edge and avoided eye contact with the people around us. Adam lingered, wiping water from his face as he watched me.

"I'll be there in a minute," he said.

I nodded and padded with wet socks across the grass. I was sitting beside our cubby, tugging on my shoes, when he approached. He'd taken off his shirt and was wringing it out. I let my attention drift to his abs, where the pale scar ran across the bottom of his abdomen.

"You got me in trouble," I said.

"You got yourself in trouble." He raked a hand through his hair, pushing it off his brow, and slid on his shoes. After he grabbed our phones and gave me mine, he smiled. "So, do I have to ask you to be my girlfriend or did you get the point?"

"I got the point, Meade. I got it loud and clear."

14

Tell

"I'm not sleeping," my dad said through the dark.

"It's just me," I answered, shutting the hotel door.

He blinked at me, barely able to keep his eyes open. He was pushed up on his forearms, but he was still half-asleep.

"Have fun?" he mumbled, flopping back into his pillows.

"Yes."

He grumbled something inaudible as I tiptoed across the room. He was snoring before I managed to get a fresh change of clothes from the duffel. I sneaked into the bathroom and flipped on the light. I looked like a rainbow, with multihued paint dried in my hair, on my face, and coated to the black Pader High shirt.

While I stripped, steam coated the room like a thick fog and stole my reflection. I stepped beneath the hot water, and the paint dripped to the tiled floor, washing away the night.

Adam and I were a thing.

My heart pounded as a smile graced my face. He'd come out of nowhere, but it felt right. Everything felt like it was finally falling into place. My phone beeped, and I poked my head around the shower curtain. On the counter, the screen glowed with a text notification. I washed the rest of the paint off before getting out.

The floor was frigid against my feet, but it didn't compare to the chill that racked through me when I saw:

Seth: Why are you at Auburn?

Confused, my fingers clenched around the phone. I scoured for any way he could've known, and an eerie feeling settled in my gut. When I went to Facebook, the proof was evident. Adam had tagged me in a picture of us covered in paint. He had also sent a relationship request, which I'd yet to accept.

The phone buzzed again.

Seth: Call me please

I sucked in a breath and turned off the screen. I would handle this in the morning, when I wasn't exhausted and riding a high from the events of the night.

My hair soaked the collar of a clean tee, and I pulled a comb through it. After brushing my teeth and finishing the rest of my nightly routine, I collected my clothes. The blue Auburn bracelet I wore, the one that matched Seth's, remained on the counter. I took it in my palm, let my fingers trace the letters one last time, then tossed it in the trash.

I reentered the main room and walked across the scratchy

carpet. Tucked beneath the heavy blankets, I put the phone on my charger, then watched the red light of the smoke detector flicker on and off. It was my version of counting sheep, and it lullabied me to sleep when my brain refused to shut off.

"Claire," my dad called through the pitch-black room.

I stirred.

"Claire," he repeated.

My phone vibrated on the nightstand, clanking against the metal lamp.

"Answer it or shut it off," my dad continued.

Groggy, I flung my hand into the frigid air and searched for the source. The phone stopped ringing as soon as I made contact.

"Hello?" I said.

"Hello?" a guy's voice repeated.

"Yeah," I answered. "What do you need?"

"Claire."

My name, said the way I'd heard it for two long years, heated me as if a fire was lit beneath the comforter. My chest grew heavy. My stomach curled. I shouldn't have answered the phone.

"Claire," Seth repeated.

I pulled the phone away from my face to confirm what I already knew. When I put it back to my ear, he released a sharp sigh.

"I can hear you breathing," he said. His tone was deep, but his accent was gruff—like it was after football games. Like he'd been out with our friends, celebrating. "The least you can do is answer me."

"I don't have to answer you," I replied. "You lost that privilege a long time ago."

"Claire," my dad muttered. "My head is pounding. Go talk in the bathroom."

"I have to go," I relayed into the phone. "Have a good night."

"Claire, wait—"

I ended the call and turned off the phone. I wouldn't make that mistake again.

* * *

The morning came quicker than I wanted. Dizzy from lack of sleep and filled with feelings that conflicted each other, I watched the sun through the sheer curtains and deleted Seth's attempts at communication.

There were texts after I'd hung up, texts I didn't want to read, and they blared at me from the phone like a harbinger of doom.

"You look like death warmed over," Adam said.

I shut the door and forced a smile. We'd gotten back around one in the morning, but somehow Adam managed to look normal. He kept his stubble, but his hair was gelled away from his face, and he wore a white polo with dark blue jeans. Absent were the bags I wore. Absent was anything that resembled exhaustion. I was slumming it up in sweats, and he looked like a model. Whatever. At least I was comfortable.

"I need coffee," I answered. "If you're here this early, I demand coffee."

"I can see you're a morning person."

"Coffee," I snapped.

"Right! Coffee it is."

We found the downstairs lobby, where the smell of bacon and eggs drifted from the back of the room. Adam headed straight for the food while I searched for coffee. I spotted two industrial-sized urns at the back of the room and navigated through the tables.

"They have bagels!" Adam said, meeting me beside the urn. He held a plate of food and grabbed one from the middle. "Cinnamon is my favorite," he said, taking a big whiff.

I grabbed a disposable cup from the stack and pressed the release button on the urn. It sputtered but refused to give me caffeine. That was okay. There was another urn of . . .

DECAF?

"No. No. Nooooo."

I tried the first urn again, but nothing came out. Panicked, I shook the urn and pushed the button again.

Adam's hand rested on my shoulder, and I spun, sending him and his bagels backward. One glance at me, and he tucked his plate to his chest.

"Your face is red," he said. "Why?"

"Coffee," I whispered, pointing at the urn. "There isn't any. Why isn't there coffee?!"

Adam glanced around the room like he was seeking the quickest escape route. When his eyes settled on the main entrance, he handed me his plate. "Hold these."

"Bagels don't replace coffee," I argued.

"I realize that."

He shook the plate, and I took it. He took a step back. "Don't eat them. They're mine. I'll be right back."

"But . . . coffee . . ."

"I'll be right back," he repeated.

He ignored my protest and walked out of the room, leaving me standing beside the empty coffee urn with a cloudy mind and a plate full of bagels. When he returned, I'd stolen one.

"That's my cinnamon bagel!" he said.

"And you're right, it's delicious."

He narrowed his eyes and pulled his hand from behind his back. Tight in his grasp was a portable cup with a lid on it. "Well, I was going to give you this," he answered, "but I don't know if you deserve it now."

"Adam," I said, trying to keep my composure, "give me the coffee or I'll throw your bagels on the ground."

"Not the bagels!"

I shifted the plate so the bagels slid to the rim. "Please don't make me do this. It'll hurt you and me both."

"But they're innocent bystanders."

"A girl has to do what a girl has to do."

He rolled his eyes and handed me the cup. "Fine," he agreed. "Rain on my parade."

"Gladly." I sipped the caffeine and relished its bitter taste. It wasn't Starbucks, but it was strong enough to shake my exhaustion.

"I sent you a Facebook request," he said, watching me as I raised the cup again. "You okay with us going public?"

"Yeah," I answered.

I grinned and pulled my phone from the pocket of my hoodie. Adam's request was accepted in less than two seconds, and Riley texted me in less than five.

"They know," I said, flashing him the text.

"Good. Let them."

* * *

The noonday sun hung high in the sky by the time we reached campus and Jordan-Hare Stadium. My dad and Adam had meetings scheduled all afternoon. They met the coaches outside the stadium, and I pivoted, passing the field where the neon run had been the night before.

The Student Center wasn't far. I found an empty table on the patio and worked on makeup homework while I waited. Case called me halfway through a math assignment. I welcomed the distraction.

"Didn't think you got up this early on the weekends," I said.

"Mom made me mow. I didn't have a choice."

I chuckled and closed my book. "She driving you crazy?"

"Yes," he answered. "I've taken out three loads of trash, helped pull the fall decorations from the attic, and was forced to be the taste tester for something she called eggplant lasagna. When you coming home? I need you here to distract her."

"We fly out tomorrow," I replied. "Think our plane lands around two."

"Can't wait." He paused, and I heard a door close. "How's the trip with Meade? Saw you two were official. Thanks for texting me and letting me know. I see how I rank on your need-to-know list."

"It was early," I said. "I was doing you a favor by letting you sleep in."

"I sleep like the dead. A text wouldn't have woken me. You know that."

"My bad."

"Yeah, your bad," he said. "So, what happened? How did this go from a football trip to a Claire-and-Adam-get-together trip? Does Dad know? And what was with that picture of you two covered in paint?"

"Dad doesn't know it's official. He knows we went out last

night, but he doesn't know the specifics. This is still a football trip. The pair of them are at the stadium right now. What was your last question?"

"I thought you were going to watch him," Case replied.

"That wasn't a question," I answered. He sighed, and I relaxed into my chair. "I can feel you judging me from North Carolina. Unless you want me judging *your* social life, get your nose out of mine."

"You can do what you want, Claire, but I'm the one who has to watch you mope around the house when it doesn't work out. I'm also the one on a team with him. I don't want to feel obligated to throat-punch him if he breaks you. Pretty sure that would be a morale crusher."

"I'm a big girl," I said. "If it doesn't work out, I'll pick myself off the ground like I did the last time. It'll suck, but I can survive Adam. I survived Seth, didn't I?"

"Have you heard from Seth?"

"Have *you* heard from him?" I replied. Case hesitated. I knew the answer before he admitted it. "Did he call you last night?" I asked, my stomach churning.

"Yeah," Case answered.

I sighed and squeezed the bridge of my nose. A headache lurked behind my temple, the consequence of too little sleep and too much stress.

"Does Adam know you two planned on going to Auburn together?" Case continued.

I paled and nausea rose in my throat. That was something only the pair of us knew. Seth and I had agreed on Auburn. We wanted to stay together, experience college together, but things changed. I changed. Now my allegiance to Auburn lay solely with my grandpa's love of it—*my* love of it. Seth was out of the picture.

"Because I'm assuming he doesn't know," Case continued.

"He doesn't."

"Then you need to tell him before he finds out. Seth still plans on going there. At least according to the drunken ramblings I got last night. That has the potential to make things a little messy, don't you think?"

"Yeah," I said. "If the situation was reversed, I'd want to know."

"Then tell him," Case repeated.

I nodded and glanced at the stadium again. Adam needed to know, but not now—not when we'd bridged the space between us and were finally on the same page.

"I've got to go," I said. "I'll text you tomorrow. Okay?"

"Tell Adam," Case answered.

"I will."

I'm Here

"Why didn't you tell him?"

"Because I didn't," I grumbled.

My duffel hit the bed and I turned. Case stood in my doorway, his arms crossed as he surveyed me. My nerves were already on edge from trying to figure out how to tell Adam. I didn't need Case worsening the situation.

"I couldn't do it," I said. "Not when we had a plane ride ahead of us. If Adam got pissed, there'd be nowhere to go. We'd be stuck together, high above the ground. Do you know how awkward that would be?"

"Claire." Case raked a hand over his face and shook his head. "I can't with you right now."

"Don't get mad at me," I said. "I should be mad at *you* for talking to my ex."

"Seth was my friend before he was your ex. Besides, I was asleep when he called. What's your excuse?"

"I was asleep, too," I answered.

"You can't steal my excuse."

"But it was the same for both of us."

Case pivoted and stepped into the hallway. "This has disaster written all over it," he grumbled. "I want no part of it. Seth's number is getting blocked. Keep whatever goes on between you and Adam far away from me."

"Case."

His door closed with a slam, and I flung myself onto the bed, my eyes finding the ceiling as if the answers were etched in the paint. Secrets weren't the way to start a relationship, but neither were complications.

* * *

Almost two weeks later, guilt weighed my conscience. I couldn't carry on while my past gnawed at my future. I had to say something; I had to be honest and hope the truth wouldn't root itself between Adam and me.

I worked on game stats, my breath catching as the clock wound down to zero. Rain cascaded in a veil of mist that saturated the turf. Our linemen placed gloved hands to the ground.

"Red, forty-eight. Red, forty-eight. Set. Hut."

Adam received the snap and shuffled backward, his eyes darting side to side as his best friend sprinted down the field. Tate was closing the gap to the end zone, but he was too covered by the defense to make a completion. There was no way Adam could get the ball there without it being intercepted.

To the left, a defensive tackle broke the line and charged at him. Adam moved out of the pocket, handing the ball to a running back, who pivoted and slid through a small gap in the defense. He sprinted downfield, bypassing players that tried to catch him. By the time Tate's coverage got to the other side of the field, it was too late. Our player was already in the end zone.

Excitement crackled through the air, amplified when special teams took the field and sealed our win, but the victory wasn't as sweet. Until I could get my head on the present, everything would be tainted.

The stands emptied, and arms wrapped around me in a hug. My mom stood behind me with a huge foam finger and every piece of Pader High clothing she could find.

"Where's your dad?" she asked, releasing me as she scanned the sidelines.

"On the field."

She latched on to my arm as we navigated the crowd. Adam stood in the end zone, his helmet tucked under his arm as soaked strands of hair clung to his forehead. My dad stood beside him, smiling as they talked with people decked in collegiate gear.

"UNC would like you to visit as soon as possible," one of the guys said. We stopped a few feet over to give them privacy, but their conversation was easily overheard.

"Don't get ahead of yourself," interjected another guy, wearing a crimson-and-white polo. "Alabama grabbed last year's national championship. We're on track to win again."

"You're playing LSU Saturday," the UNC coach pointed out. "They'll knock you off number one."

"Worry about your own game," Alabama's coach replied. He looked at Adam again, smiling beneath his umbrella. "I heard you recently visited one of our rivals. Come back to Alabama. You won't be disappointed."

"Yes, sir."

The coach patted Adam on the shoulder, and I waited, smiling despite the knot in my throat. I didn't want to wreck his happiness, but I was worried.

"Hi, dear," Wanda said, greeting me as my mom stepped away to talk to Riley's parents. Wanda wore a poncho, but her face was sallow beneath the hood's yellow vinyl. Her icy fingers wrapped around my forearm. I covered them and glanced at Adam. He remained in conversation with the UNC scout.

"More colleges?" she asked, her gaze following mine.

"UNC," I said. "Alabama was there a little bit ago, but they're gone now. I think Adam was interested."

She stumbled backward, her thin fingers becoming limp as her eyes rolled to the back of her head. I caught her before she hit the ground.

"Adam!"

People crowded around as I slumped to the ground beneath Wanda's weight.

"Wanda," I said, fear holding my heart as Adam screamed to let him through. "Wanda? Wanda."

* * *

I hated hospitals.

The smell of antiseptic carried through miles of halls, the dull citrus smell marred by the stench of stale cafeteria food. The walls were white, their monotonous decor broken only by the occasional poster. Each room beeped from machines inside. The repetitive sound of heart monitors was disrupted only by nurses and doctors as they entered and exited the rooms.

My experience with hospitals was limited, but every visit was the same. Put on a smile, act like everything is okay, and leave wondering if that was good-bye. In a place filled with lifelines, the only thing I could think about was death. I felt awful for being like that, especially now.

I bought a water from the vending machine and crossed the tiled floor. Visiting hours were over. They'd been over since we arrived with the ambulance, but Adam asked me to stay. He was too torn up to leave alone, so my parents sought a hotel in Charlotte while we waited for news.

Nurses sat behind their station, filling out charts and typing on the computer. They gave me a nod of acknowledgment as I turned toward Wanda's room. Adam stood outside the door, talking to the doctor. I slowed, trying to decide whether to wait in the waiting room or carry on.

"We'll check her in the morning," the doctor said, a folder in his hand. "Once we get a scan, we'll know."

Adam nodded and pushed a hand through his hair. His eyes met mine as the doctor stepped away. He had changed into street clothes as soon as Wanda was admitted, but he was the same scared guy who'd rushed to the sidelines with his grandma in his arms.

"How is she?" I asked.

"Worse than she's been," he answered. He paused, shaking his head. "She has leukemia, Claire."

Dread flooded my veins.

"We found out right after school started."

"I'm so sorry."

He shifted the weight on his feet and scratched the back of his neck, his eyes on the floor. "She's been on chemo, but it's been rougher on her than the cancer. Right now, they want to do a scan. If it has spread too far, we have to decide if—"

A V creased the space between his brows, and his eyes burned red, brimming with tears that spilled over his cheeks in a steady stream.

"Claire, she's the only family I have. What am I supposed to do?"

I wrapped him in a hug as he crumbled outside Wanda's hospital room. I didn't have the answers. I couldn't do anything but try and hold together pieces that splintered off and crashed to the floor.

Adam pulled away, swiping his hands under his eyes. "I need to pull myself together," he said, his voice wracked with emotion. "I'm sorry."

"Don't apologize to me," I answered.

My phone buzzed, and he blew a steady breath. When I handed him the water, he twisted the cap and took a long swig. I glanced at my phone, my mom's name crossing the screen.

"You should go," he said as he closed the bottle.

"I don't want you to be alone."

"I'll be fine." He handed me the water, but I shook my head. "I'll call you first thing in the morning and let you know if anything's changed," he said, grabbing my hand as we found the elevator. "Can you call Tate for me? My phone is dead, but he'll want to know what's going on."

"You can use my phone."

Adam shook his head. "I don't want to rehash everything that's happened tonight. Just tell him I'm fine and to focus on this week's game. I don't want to come back to a team that's forgotten how to block and a receiver who doesn't remember the plays. This is my last year to get to state. We're bringing that trophy home one way or the other."

"Football can wait," I answered.

"Just because I'm here doesn't mean the world stopped spinning."

We entered the elevator, and the doors slid shut. Adam tugged me to him, his hands finding the small of my back. He looked exhausted as he lowered his forehead to mine and let out a ragged sigh.

"I'm here if you need me," I told him. "Just call. I'll be here as fast as a car will take me."

"I will." He kissed me as the elevator jolted to a stop and slid open to the main floor.

We walked to the exit, pausing to let the security guard know Adam would be right back. Once we stepped into the cool October night, my parents greeted us.

"We'll be back in the morning," my dad said. "Try to get some sleep between now and then. Okay? Getting overly exhausted won't help anyone."

"Yes, sir." Adam nodded. My mom pulled him in for a hug. Once she released him, he reached for me. "I'll text you later," he said, his arms strong around my waist.

"Let me know if anything changes," I answered, nestling against his chest and hugging him tight. "You're not alone. Remember that."

"I know. See you tomorrow, Collins."

"Good night, Meade."

Fate

Terminal.

Worries about Seth, worries about college, everything paled in comparison to Wanda's eight-letter diagnosis. The doctors gave her until June and said they would do everything in their power to postpone the inevitable. Wanda was ready to fight. She would always fight.

"Thought you were headed to Charlotte," my mom said, glancing at me from the kitchen.

"Thought you were headed to the game," I answered.

I paused in our living room and searched for my sunglasses. I had told Adam I would stop by the hospital on my way to the game, but it was too bright to make the trip without them.

"Have you seen my sunglasses?" I asked, staring at my mom as she straightened her bedazzled jersey. "I thought I left them in here."

"Check your room."

I found them beside my laptop, where my Alabama application was still visible on the screen. The application was halfway completed, and I felt like I was cheating on Auburn by even entertaining the idea.

"Claire!" my mom called from the kitchen. "You've got something in the mail!"

I slid the sunglasses over my hair and took the stairs two at a time. My mom was standing in the kitchen, leaning against the island.

"Something you want to tell me?" she said, smiling as she showed me a blue envelope.

I rushed across the floor, emotions swelling as I spotted the AU logo at the top. *Welcome to the Family* was written beneath the logo.

"I've been so busy, I haven't even thought about checking my application," I said, ripping the letter from inside.

> *Dear Claire,*
> *Welcome to Auburn University!*

"I got in," I said, quiet at first. My eyes burned as I stared at my mom. Tears streamed down her cheeks. "I got in!" I repeated, louder. "Mom, I got in! I got in!"

She hugged me and we jumped up and down.

"I got in!" I said again, handing her the letter and pulling out the rest of the information.

"You got in," she repeated.

I patted my pocket, searching for my phone. I had to tell my dad. I had to tell Case. Adam. Adam, I needed to tell in person. He would be excited for me, but I needed to do it face-to-face.

I hit the home button on my phone. A text was waiting.

Seth: I got in

Anxiety washed over me like waves on a sandcastle, pulling my excitement out to sea and leaving the remnants destroyed in the sand.

"You okay?" my mom asked, reaching for the rest of the information.

"Yeah," I lied. I forced a smile and cleared the text. "Going to call Dad on my way to Charlotte. I'll text you when I get there."

"You telling your brother, too?"

"Yeah, after the game."

She hugged me again, her arms tight around me like she didn't want to let go. "You're going to do great," she said, her voice shaky. "I'm going to miss you, and I'm going to call you every day, but I'm so incredibly proud of you. I love you."

"I love you, too."

Backpack on my shoulder and sunglasses on my head, I stepped into the afternoon and stared at the azure sky. If fate was up there, taunting me, I needed it to switch to my side.

I drove to Charlotte, begging the universe to let Seth's Auburn acceptance be a lie. Maybe this was his way of getting my attention? I shook my head, knowing that wasn't the truth. Seth was a jerk, but he never slacked on his grades. If he wanted to get into Auburn, he could've.

Everything about this made my stomach churn. I had to tell Adam. Now there wasn't any other choice.

Dusk shot a mix of colors across the sky and reflected off the hospital's large glass windows. I pulled into a parking space at the front and texted Adam before turning off the car.

Claire: I'm here. Good luck tonight!

He'd be too preoccupied with the game to see the text until later, but it eased my guilt. I couldn't remedy the Seth situation in an instant, but at least this way I felt like I was focusing on Adam.

I crammed the phone in my pocket and crossed through the cars. When I found Wanda's room, the smell of bland soup hung in the air. I scrunched my nose as she waved me in.

"Tell me you brought contraband," she said, letting the too-thin mixture drip off her spoon. I shook my head, and she frowned. "If I give you a dollar, would you run to the vending machine and sneak me a Snickers?"

"The doctor has your sugar intake limited, but I'll check for trail mix."

"You're my favorite," she answered. "Don't tell Adam or I'll deny it."

She shifted against the pillows while I took a seat on the couch and glanced at the television. An old Western was on the screen. She turned it off and smiled.

"Tell me about the outside world," she said. "Any juicy gossip?"

"No juicy gossip," I said, "but I come bearing gifts." I dug into my backpack and pulled out a small electronic. Wanda's brow furrowed until I turned it around.

"My lands," she whispered.

"Electronic Scrabble," I said, leaning so she could take the gift. "Didn't think they were still around, but I found one on-line. Figured it would be a good distraction for when Adam and I are at school."

Wanda lowered her glasses so they sat on the tip of her nose. The machine beeped to life, and she grinned. "I feel like a child on Christmas morning. Thank you, dear."

"You're welcome."

She fiddled with the game for a minute, and I looked at my phone.

"How's school?" she asked.

"Long," I answered. "We have semester exams in a few weeks, so all the teachers are trying to cram information before then. Most days I feel like banging my head on the desk. Otherwise, it's not that bad."

"Adam doing okay in school?"

"He's doing okay in the class we share," I replied. "Can't speak for his other classes, but he seems like he's caught up."

"Good." She blew out an exhale and relaxed into the pillows. "I worry about him and how this affects his school. Your dad is doing such a wonderful job helping him with football and scholarships, but none of it matters if he doesn't keep those grades up."

"I don't think you have to worry about him," I said. "Adam's pretty set on playing college football. He wouldn't do anything to jeopardize his chances."

She nodded. "He was talking about Clemson and Alabama the other day, so I got the nurse to help me look them up. They looked like nice schools, but he said he'd bring me an information packet as soon as he picks. They still send those, don't they, dear?"

"Depends on the school. Some send info, but others send instructions for how to find the information online."

"Well, you're a smart girl. Which would you pick?"

"Either is fine," I said.

They weren't the schools of my choice, but they were still good schools. If Adam was dead set on not going to Auburn, those were two football programs he'd do well in.

Goose bumps spread along my skin, brought by nerves and the frigid temperature of Wanda's room. I raked a hand over my arm, seeing her brow tug together as she straightened in the bed.

"Are you two looking at the same schools?" she asked.

"Not exactly," I said. "I'm going to Auburn."

"That's where you two went with your dad, right?"

"Yes, ma'am."

"And remind me, where was it?"

"Alabama."

She paused, mischief clear behind her green eyes.

"He'll pick the best school for him," I said. "If that's Alabama, great. If it's Clemson, great. Who knows, he might stay in North Carolina and surprise us all."

"Do you want him to go to Alabama?"

"It doesn't matter, does it?"

There was a small knock on the door, and the doctor pushed it open. He glanced at Wanda, then me, then back. "Ready for respiratory therapy?" he asked, grabbing a plastic thing with a blue hose attached.

Wanda didn't look thrilled. "Thought once was enough," she said, scowling.

"Once was enough, three days ago," he replied. "We upped your therapy to three times daily, remember?"

"I'm going on a food run," I said, winking at her as I approached the door.

Wanda's face softened momentarily, but hardened as she glared at the doctor again. I shut the door and stepped into the hall.

I found a vending machine near the lobby. Trail mix wasn't an option, so I continued to the ground floor. The makeshift store near the cafeteria had a decent selection. I scanned the labels for the one with the least amount of sugar and headed to the register. My phone rang as the cashier scanned my stuff.

Seth.

I groaned and handed the worker a ten-dollar bill. I was cramming the change in my pocket when he called again.

My blood heated, and my hand clenched around the phone. We couldn't do this forever, and he couldn't take silence for a hint. I was done being patient.

"This has to stop," I hissed into the phone, finding a chair as isolated as I could. "When I don't answer you, it's because I don't want to talk to you! Leave me alone."

"I miss you," he said, his deep voice curling around the words in a way that used to make me swoon.

Not anymore.

I shook my head. "No, you don't get the right to miss me. You broke up with me. Now you get to move on and enjoy your free-dom. Remember?"

"I can't move on," he said, sighing. "I made a mistake, Claire. I want to fix this before it's too late."

"It is too late. I have a boyfriend, Seth. Go find someone and be happy."

"You make me happy."

"Then you shouldn't have broken my heart." Anger swept through me. "You should've tried long distance. You should've tried something!"

"I was stupid."

"Yeah, you were." I turned the bag of trail mix in my free hand. "Whatever we were . . . it's in the past," I said. "Please let it go and move on. I did."

"Do you love him?"

I hesitated as adrenaline tingled through me. When I moved to Pader, Adam was the last thing I wanted. I hadn't expected any of this, but that didn't change how I felt.

"Do you love him?" Seth repeated.

"Yeah," I answered. "I do."

Seth started to reply, but I hung up the phone before his words were all the way out. I needed nothing more from him. I, Claire Collins, was in love with Adam Meade. For now, that's all I needed.

17

Thank You

"You need to be back by ten," Case said, crossing his ankles atop the coffee table. "Ten-o-one and I'm ratting you out."

"Don't be jealous I have a date, and you're stuck here."

"Hook me up with Riley, and I'd have a date."

"She's not interested," I said, opening the front door. "I'd have better luck hooking you up with a nun."

"Dream crusher!"

I stepped outside as Adam shut his truck door. He closed the distance and kissed me without pause. For the first time in a while, we weren't occupied with football or hospital visits. He was the only person who existed in my world, and I was the only one who existed in his.

"What are you doing the rest of the night?" he asked, his mouth quirking upward as he pulled his face away.

"Why? Are you trying to get me in trouble?"

His smile widened, and I glanced at the house. My parents were at the Booster Club meeting across town, and Case wouldn't bug me unless it was an emergency. My options were open.

"I'm up for whatever," I said, "but you'd better have me home before ten. My parents will blow a gasket if I miss curfew."

"Noted."

His feet crunched over loose gravel, and the passenger side door creaked open. I slid inside as our porch light turned on.

Two houses down, staked to the ground with spotlights on them, Riley's yard held painted turkeys and a HAPPY THANKS-GIVING sign. I glanced at the decorations as Adam hurried down the street, passing Tate's Mustang parked outside.

"He's accepting an offer from UNC," Adam said, indicating the car.

"Really?"

Adam nodded, his eyes on the road. "He texted me earlier. Said your dad got the call this afternoon and talked to him about it. I'm happy for him. It's a good program."

"But Riley applied to the University of South Carolina," I answered. "They decide to try long distance?"

"I think Tate's hoping she'll change her mind. Long distance rarely works, even for a couple as solid as them."

Concerned, I glanced at Adam. Long distance was the only way we could stay together and go to separate colleges. If he didn't think long distance was doable, we had a problem.

"You're not into trying long distance?" I asked.

"Are you?"

I shrugged and looked at the sidewalk through the window. Orange leaves riffled in the breeze, swept away by darkness and a season they couldn't control. Tension filled the truck as we rode the rest of the way in silence. When we reached his house, Adam pulled into the driveway and parked.

"What's up?" he asked, his brow furrowed. "Why do you look like that?"

"I look like nothing," I replied. I pushed open the truck's door, but Adam caught up with me before I reached the yard.

"I know you better than that," he said. "What's going on?"

"Nothing," I repeated.

"Claire." He blocked the sidewalk and towered over me like a statue in the dark. His jaw clenched as his eyes scanned my face. "I can't read your mind," he said, "and I don't have the energy for this. Tell me what's wrong."

"You wouldn't even try long distance, would you?" I asked, my words muffled by the sound of leaves scraping across the pavement.

"Do you really think it would work?"

"Maybe."

He sighed and scratched his jaw. "I've never been in a position where I had to think about the possibility of long distance," he said, "and it's not something we need to worry about right now. I still have colleges to tour, and you might decide to change your mind. Who knows, maybe the decision will be made for you. Maybe it won't even be an issue."

I took a step back, trying to register what I hoped he hadn't said. "I'm sorry," I answered, holding up a hand to halt him. "Did you just imply that maybe I won't get into Auburn?" He frowned, and I shook my head, feeling the sting of unspoken betrayal. If he didn't think I could get in, he didn't deserve to know I was accepted. "How dare you."

"I wasn't trying to make you mad," he said, his tone turning sharp. "I just meant keep your options open. Get a backup plan in case something goes wrong."

"In case I don't get in?!" My fists balled at my sides. "That's a real dick thing to say, Adam! How would you feel if I said maybe you wouldn't get a football offer? Or, maybe you'll tear up your knee and end your football career for good?"

"That's not fair," Adam answered, his tone softer than before. "I wasn't saying you wouldn't get in. I'm sure you will. You're smart. You know that." He pivoted and stalked to the front door, his footsteps echoing off the porch as he sifted through his keys. "I don't even know how we got to this point. I told you about Tate and Riley, and somehow it turned into an argument between us. What am I missing? How did we get here?"

"Well, you started by attacking long-distance relationships. Then you pretty much said I may not get into Auburn. You're at two strikes, and you're working toward a third."

"What do you want me to say?" He pushed open the door and stepped into the dark. The light in the entrance flickered on. "I already told you I wasn't trying to piss you off with the Auburn thing. All I want is for you to keep your bases covered. If Auburn works out, great. If it doesn't, have a backup plan. As far as long-distance relationships go, I won't sugarcoat what I think of them. Nine out of ten times, they don't work. You may not like it, but that's how I feel."

"I feel like you're being a jerk," I said.

"I feel like you're being unreasonable." He moved into the kitchen, ignoring me as I remained cross-armed in the entrance. "You want ice cream?" he asked, poking his head around the corner. "I bought some from the store yesterday."

"You just ate."

"And now I'm eating again. Come in here so I can stare at you while I scoop. If you want to stay mad at me, fine. Just do it with me here. I don't want to miss out."

I entered the kitchen. He smiled at me as I walked through the door.

"I hate it when you do that," I said, scowling at him as he grabbed two bowls.

"Hate it when I do what?"

"That," I said, motioning at him. "You go from pissed to happy in point five seconds. It isn't fair."

He grinned and placed the bowls on the counter. After scooping a decent helping into both, he returned the ice cream to the freezer and licked the spoon before tossing it into the sink.

"Life isn't fair," he said, cornering me against the counter. "But we deal with it and move on. This is something we have to deal with, but we don't have to deal with it right now. Let's move on."

"What if I don't want to?" I said, looping my hands around his neck.

"Would it help if I said please?" His teeth scraped the space between my neck and my ear and I arched into him.

"I have to be home soon," I answered, feeling his hand move along my spine. "I have a test in English tomorrow, and I still have to study."

"What if I volunteered to help you?" he replied.

"Then maybe I'd take you up on your offer." His mouth tugged upward, and he kissed me. "Okay," I said. "I'll definitely take you up on your offer."

"Good answer."

He kissed me again, this time rougher, and I tugged on the hair at the base of his neck. His hair had grown shaggy and was in desperate need of a cut, but the curls at the end made it easy to twine my fingers through the strands.

"We have to talk about this eventually," I said, pausing.

"I know," he agreed, "but not tonight."

He pulled away, took our bowls, and headed to the living room. I followed, grabbing the remote from the coffee table as he took a spot on the couch.

"Been meaning to ask you," I said, taking the bowl he handed my way, "you going to the hospital on Thanksgiving or do you plan on staying in town?"

"I'll be there some of the day," he answered, looking at me as he took a bite. "Why? You want to do something?"

"We can. My mom usually does dinner, and I'm free after that. Most of the family will be there—including, but not limited to, my hipster cousins and my uncle Phil. You can come if you want, but you'll probably get a ton of questions about football. We usually watch a game or two. Phil thinks he's an ESPN analyst. Sure he'll bug you about prospects, stats, and everything in between."

"Phil sounds like my kind of guy," Adam answered, nodding. "I'll head to Charlotte early that day so I can do lunch with my grandma beforehand."

"Sounds perfect."

"Yeah." He took another bite of ice cream, his attention flickering to the bowl as he pushed the spoon around it. "Claire," he said, looking up. The features of his face were softer, almost sad, as he gave me a small smile. "Thank you for including me in your family stuff. It's been a while since I've been in a group setting like that. It really means a lot."

"Anytime."

He went back to eating, but I hesitated, my mind stewing on the words. Where was the rest of his family? Was it really just him and Wanda?

"Adam," I said, drawing his attention. "Can I ask you a personal question?"

He nodded.

"Where are your mom and dad?"

He paused and looked up from his bowl, the spoon clutched between his thumb and index finger. The green in his eyes looked less vibrant, almost wistful. He cleared his throat and set the spoon in the bowl and the bowl on the table.

"I'm not trying to pry," I said. "You just . . . you said what you did about it being a while since you've been in a group setting like that and I—"

"You're fine," he answered. "We would've talked about it eventually. It's not like I keep it a secret." He sighed and raked his hands through his messy brown hair, his eyes on me. "Can I take you somewhere?"

"Yeah."

"Then grab your coat. It's going to be cold."

18

Revelations

Throughout the ride, Adam didn't say much. I didn't know where we were going, nor did I ask. I just held his hand as he pulled off Pader's main road and passed through a large iron gate with a sign that read PADER CEMETERY. My stomach knotted.

He slowed as we turned down a narrow road. Leaves fell from the surrounding trees, tombstones littered the ground beside us, and mausoleums were lit by moonlight.

When he stopped and put the truck in park, he looked at me. "Are you scared?" he asked.

"Should I be?"

He shook his head and pushed open his door. He grabbed a flashlight from beneath the back seat and walked to my side. Out of the truck, I rubbed my arms against the brisk November breeze and took his hand once more.

He looked at me as his flashlight penetrated the dark. "I know this isn't what you expected," he started. "We can leave. I won't take it personally."

"I'm fine," I answered, gripping his hand tighter.

He walked ahead of me, and I followed, crossing over the neatly trimmed grass covered with leaves. We were careful to avoid the spaces where others lay. The air around us was still as we passed row after row, our footsteps crunching through the night.

When Adam finally stopped, he shone the beam on the tombstone in front of us. *Thomas A. Meade* became visible, along with a date and the etching *Loving father, husband, son, and friend.*

I stood there, staring at the name as Adam stood silent beside me. When he spoke, his words broke my heart.

"Claire, this is my dad. Dad, this is Claire."

His voice broke, and he let out a long exhale. The idea of Adam enduring a life without his father made my heart ache. I couldn't survive if I'd lost my dad. My whole world would be destroyed.

"And this is Avery," he said, barely getting out the words as the beam reflected off the marble tombstone to his left. "She was my little sister." He tore his attention away, his eyes brimming with tears.

It felt like someone had put a ten-pound weight on my chest, pressing the breath from my lungs and leaving me with no way to breathe. Tears burned down my cheeks as he continued.

"There was a storm," he said. "It was my mom's birthday, and the three of us went to the store to grab a cake. It was supposed to be a surprise—we were so excited to get her a surprise—but on the way back, my dad hit a wet patch in the road. The police said our car wrapped around a tree. Dad and Avery died on impact, and I barely made it out alive. I was the only one who . . ."

I turned and wrapped my arms around his waist, trying to do something other than stand there. I wanted to will away his sadness, to erase this horrible tragedy from his past, but I was helpless. All I could do was hug him. All I could do was be there.

"My mom had a breakdown when I was twelve," Adam said, his voice so quiet I could barely hear. "She got involved with some stuff she shouldn't have and was supposed to go to rehab. My grandma took over at that point. It was a temporary arrangement, until my mom got out and adjusted, but she left rehab within a couple of weeks and OD'd a week later. She's buried up north, where her family wanted her. Grandma and I didn't get a say."

I nestled my head against his chest and breathed in his scent. This wasn't fair. His parents should've been here, his sister should've been here. I buried the thought of life without Case. I wouldn't be able to cope. Nothing could heal a loss like that.

"Tell me what you're thinking," Adam whispered, his chin coming to rest on the crown of my head. "You're being quiet, and I'm worried. You're never quiet."

"I didn't know," I said. "I wouldn't have asked if I had any idea."

"You needed to know." His thumbs swept the tears off my cheeks, the movement tender and warm. "I know what it's like to love someone and lose them, and I know what it's like to try and come back from that. It takes everything you have to go on, every piece of strength you can get, and it's exactly why I don't get attached. Why I didn't get attached."

"You're afraid of losing people."

"Yeah," he answered, "and now I'm afraid of losing you."

I kissed him, my hands finding the edge of his jaw, where stubble prickled my fingers. "You won't lose me," I said. "Figuring out the college situation will be a mess, but I want to make it work. I want you."

"Good, because I want you, too."

He rested his forehead against mine, and I stared into those vivid green eyes. I wanted to tell him I loved him, wanted to tell him everything, but I couldn't. I was trapped by my secrets, trapped by Seth, and now wasn't the time. All I wanted to think about was Adam.

I was a lucky girl. Luckier than I realized.

Reminders

"Are you sure you can bake?"

"I don't know. Try a piece. If you get food poisoning, the rest of us will know not to eat it."

Adam chuckled as I pulled a pie from the oven. I had given this pie my everything. People needed to appreciate my work of art before it lost its freshly baked gleam.

"Is it supposed to be runny?" he asked, leaning against the counter with his arms crossed.

"It's not runny," I answered, "and if you keep messing with me, I'll poke you in the eye with that temperature gauge. You'll spend your day at the hospital getting operated on and eating yucky food."

"Meh. The nurses at the hospital are hot, and most of them know me by name. It would be a happy Thanksgiving indeed." I cocked an eyebrow at him, and he grabbed a casserole from the island. "I think now would be a good time to bring this to the table."

"I think you're right."

He turned the corner, leaving me to my own devices. My mom had taken point on table decorating, and I was left to finish up the last of the food.

I was pulling an overcooked green bean casserole from the oven when Adam reentered the kitchen. He scanned the pan with interest, then looked at me.

"Pretty sure it's not supposed to be burned," he said, grinning.

"My mom set the timer!" I answered. He laughed as I poked the charred bits of green beans. "Maybe we could say it's a fresh take on a classic?"

"Um, maybe."

I marched to the pantry and retrieved the last of the onion crisps. If those couldn't drown out the burnt taste, oh well. At least I tried.

"How's your grandma?" I asked, opening the canister on my way back.

"She's good. Said to wish you a happy Thanksgiving, and to let you know she's got everything covered."

"She's got everything covered?" I repeated, dumping the onions over the top. "What does that mean?"

"No idea," Adam said, holding his hand out for some of the onions. "Figured you would know."

"Nope. Your guess is as good as mine."

I was finishing up the casserole when my mom rushed in, grabbing an apron from a hook near the entrance.

"Okay," she said. "I've got the table set, and everyone is here except Chloe. Where are we with food? What do I need to do?"

"The sweet potato soufflé is probably cool, and I just pulled the green bean casserole out of the oven," I answered, pulling my apron over my head. "Need me to do anything else?"

"Nope," she replied. "Just stay within earshot so I can call you when we're ready to eat."

"Will do."

I nodded at the door, and Adam followed me into the hall. On the way outside, I grabbed one of Case's old footballs from the hall closet.

"This is more my style," Adam said, clapping his hands together.

"Same. I get my cooking skills from my mom."

The November air was crisp against my cheeks and threw strands of curled brown hair in my face. I stepped off the porch, closing my sweater tighter as Adam followed behind me.

"So," he said, crossing the grass, "any way you'd be interested in making me a sign for next week's game? It's a big one!"

"Depends," I answered, taking my place across from him. "What's in it for me?"

"What's in it for you?" he repeated, throwing me the ball. I nodded and he grinned. "I'm sure I could think of some pretty cheesy thing to do. Christmas is coming up. Who knows, I might buy you a gift?"

"Speaking of which, what do you want? Currently thinking about something football related."

"It doesn't matter to me."

"Not an answer," I said. I threw the ball back to him. "I'll ask Tate for recommendations. I'm sure he can give me an idea or two."

"Totally fine with me. I've already got Riley giving me ideas." He threw the ball back to me, then glanced over his shoulder.

Tate's Mustang was parked at the curb. "Remind me to talk to him about next weekend's party. It's supposed to be Saturday, but I don't think I'll be there. My grandma's up for this clinical trial thing. Pretty sure it's the same day."

"Will do."

My phone buzzed in my pocket, and I tossed the ball back to Adam before pulling it from my pocket.

> **Seth:** Happy Thanksgiving. I know you hate me, but still hope you have a good one.

I clenched the phone harder. If this was his idea of staying relevant, he was wrong.

"Claire, Adam, dinner," my mom said, her voice carrying from the door.

Adam jogged across the lawn, leaves crunching beneath his tennis shoes. "You good there?" he asked, motioning at my phone.

"Yeah. I'm fine." I closed out the screen, shoved the phone in my pocket, and grabbed his hand. "But I'll be even more fine after I eat. Burnt casseroles and runny pies, here I come."

* * *

"Good morning, sunshine."

"Is that bacon?"

"And waffles," my dad replied.

I sniffed the kitchen, searching for the plate as he pointed a spatula at the counter. Dad's waffles were a day after Thanksgiving tradition, and I was more than happy to eat my weight in syrup.

"Do me a favor," he said. "Refill that pot of coffee. Your mom drank it all while I was mixing batter. I haven't had time to stop between waffles, but it's waffles for caffeine. No coffee, no waffles."

"I got your back," I said.

While I found the coffee pot and scooped hazelnut grounds into a filter, Case slumped through the door. He plopped onto one of the barstools, looking like a hot mess as he ran a hand across his face.

"Look what the cat dragged in," I said.

"Bacon," Case replied.

"Long night?" my dad asked.

"Yep," he groaned.

I glanced at my father, who held up a finger and grabbed the knob on the nearest cabinet. He slammed the door shut.

"Could we not go around slamming doors?" Case groaned, clutching his head in his hands.

"Nope," my dad answered, an impish look on his face. "Next time, think about this before you come home drunk."

"It was midnight Black Friday," Case said, sounding defensive, "and I had a DD."

"Black Friday is for shopping," I said, quirking a brow.

"Well, your brother decided it was for alcohol," my dad answered. He looked at Case and shook his head. "You having a DD was very responsible. Glad you made one wise decision before you threw up all over the front porch and fell asleep on the bathroom floor."

I turned on the coffee maker and fled the kitchen before I was stuck listening to the usual lecture Case was destined for. I reached the stairs as my dad launched into Full Father Mode.

Upstairs, my room was lit by rays of sunshine, and my dad's voice was drowned by the quiet undertones of acoustic music. My laptop lay open on my desk, with dormitory options visible on the screen. The admissions letter sat beside the computer, with all the accompanying information behind it in a neat little stack.

I picked up the letter and scanned the words. When my phone buzzed against the lamp on my bedside table, I put the letter back and padded barefoot across the room. Adam's name was visible on the screen.

"You've reached Claire Collins," I said, placing the phone to my ear. "Please leave your name, number, and a brief message after the beep. Beep."

"Okay," he answered, humor in his tone. "I was going to see if you wanted to hang out tonight, but it's fine. I'll just call Tate and tell him I'm up for—"

"No!" I interrupted. "I'm free and I'd love to see you. What time will you be here?"

"Um, six? Maybe. Grandma asked me to bring her some stuff from home, so I'll be up there for a while."

"That's fine. Call me when you get back."

"Awesome. See you then."

I hung up the phone and put it back on my nightstand.

"Claire!"

I shifted at Case's voice hollering from the hall. Heavy footsteps thumped against the wooden staircase, and a heavy fist beat against my door.

"Claire!" he said again.

Concerned, I pushed myself off the bed and yanked it open. Case, pale and sickly looking, was slumped against the threshold.

"Did Dad give you Pepto?" I asked.

He nodded and pointed at the stairs. "Riley's here. She looks like she—" He paused and covered his mouth. It sounded like he burped, but he turned and raced across the floor before I managed to get the rest of the sentence.

"Case?"

"Claire!" my dad hollered from the bottom of the stairs.

I peeled my eyes away from the bathroom and took the stairs two at a time. When I reached the landing, Riley stood in the living room with her back to me. She wore a black hoodie tugged over her head, black sweats, and tennis shoes. When she turned, curiosity became concern.

"What's wrong?" I asked, closing the space.

"I-I think we broke up," she said, her eyes red-rimmed. "Tate and me. I think we . . ."

I pulled her into a hug, glancing at my mom as she entered the room. "We'll be up there," I said, taking Riley by the shoulders.

We took the stairs slowly, and I closed my door as Riley stopped in the middle of the room. She sobbed a good five minutes, and I stood beside her as she wept, leftover mascara streaking down her cheeks.

"I just don't understand," she said. "We were fine, and then he—this isn't right! We were supposed to stay together."

"What happened?" I asked.

She ran the sleeve of the hoodie under her eyes and walked to my bed. I took a seat at my desk and watched her try to collect herself.

"We got in a fight," she answered. "We were supposed to go to Charlotte today, to do some early Christmas shopping." She paused. "He just started in on how nice it will be when we're at

UNC and how close to family it is. I told him we weren't going to UNC. I didn't realize he verbally committed. He gave them a verbal commitment," she repeated, looking at me. "We've been together since we were freshmen, Claire. We've talked about this, about how this is *our* decision. He didn't even tell me. He just accepted the offer and expected me to go with him. What about what I want? How is this fair?"

"It isn't fair," I answered, my heart breaking for her.

I understood where she was coming from, how one guy and one moment could flip your world upside down and tear your heart to pieces. But I survived Seth, and Riley would survive Tate. She was stronger than she knew.

"I don't know how to not be with him," she sobbed.

My phone buzzed and I stood, grabbing it from the nightstand.

Adam: Please tell me you're with Riley

Claire: I am. She's here now

I crossed my arms and let out a shaky breath. My Auburn letter glared at me from the desk. Adam and I could end up the same way. I could be the one crying, heartbroken over a guy. Watching Riley go through this was a reminder of the pain, of how easily Adam could hurt me if he chose not to see this through. I couldn't do that again. Not with Adam.

I hoped I wouldn't have to.

Trust

Darkness fell upon Pader, bringing a cold front that stirred the trees and the people around it. Adam pulled up to my house at six, looking worse for wear than I'd seen him. He met me on the sidewalk and wrapped strong arms around me, enveloping me in a cocoon of warmth.

"How's Wanda?" I asked, sliding into the truck.

"Feisty as ever," he answered. He closed the door and stepped around the hood, picking up the conversation as he got in. "She spent most of the day playing electronic Scrabble. Thanks for that. She's upped her game. Now I have zero shot at beating her."

"You're welcome."

He took my hand across the console and linked our fingers, glancing at Riley's house as we turned the corner. "How's she holding up?" he asked, returning his attention to the road.

"She's devastated."

"Yeah, so is Tate." He blew out a breath and shook his head. "They've been together for years. I never thought they'd break up like this, that a fight over colleges would be the one thing they couldn't get through. It sucks."

"Well, Tate knew Riley's plans and committed to UNC without talking to her. Maybe he should've been more considerate."

"Tate took advantage of an opportunity," Adam said. "Riley could've been more understanding." He glanced at me, his eyes lingering as we reached a stop sign. "She could still go to UNC. They have a cheer program, just like the University of South Carolina."

"Except she wants to go to South Carolina," I said, holding his gaze. "Maybe Tate could retract his verbal commitment and go there instead."

"He wants to play for UNC."

"They could do long distance."

"I don't know." Adam's gaze swept across my face, hesitating. There was a look in his eyes I couldn't place, but it wasn't warm. Something was up.

"What?" I asked.

"We need to talk about something that isn't Tate and Riley."

"Okay."

His tone held an edge I wasn't expecting, so my brow furrowed as I stared at him.

"Why did you tell my grandma I needed to go to Alabama for college?" he asked.

"What?"

"Because I don't appreciate it. She harped on me about that all afternoon."

Confused, I twisted in my seat so I could see him straight on. "I never told her I wanted you to go to Alabama. All we did was talk about your options."

"Which includes Alabama, a college that happens to be in the same state as Auburn." He pulled his hand away and wrapped it around the steering wheel. "She had a stack of info on Alabama, including dorm info, meal plan options, and undergraduate programs. I spent the rest of the day trying to hype up Clemson to her, but she wouldn't hear of it. It was Alabama this, and Alabama that, and 'Claire's going to Alabama so you should go there, too.'" He looked at me again, his lips a thin line. "Where I go to school is my decision, and I'll go wherever the hell I want. I don't need your input. I don't need you persuading my grandma, either."

I glared at him. If he wanted to throw out accusations, he needed to check the facts. "I didn't do anything wrong," I answered. "I told her I was going to Auburn. I never said where you should go."

"I don't believe you."

Tears pricked my eyes, burning the edges as they threatened to spill over. I hadn't done anything, but I was the one getting blamed!

"Talk to me," Adam said, his voice cold as the truck ascended a gravel road.

"I don't feel like talking to you right now."

He pulled the truck to a stop, and I pushed my way out, the breeze sending my hair in wayward directions as rocks crunched beneath my feet. We stood on a cliff's edge, high above Pader like two specks in a pool of star-ridden darkness. Another time, the scene would've been beautiful, but we'd wasted it with false accusations and defensiveness.

"Where I go to school is my choice," he said, coming to a stop beside me. "I thought I made that clear."

"You did make it clear. You made it crystal clear." I turned, meeting his irritated expression. "But I got into Auburn, and I'm going there with or without you."

"Is this a threat?"

"It's a promise." I pulled my jacket close to my body, needing warmth where frost now lay. "And there's something about Auburn you need to know."

"What?"

"My ex will be there, too."

Adam's face smoothed for a moment, devoid of all emotion, and my nerves stood on end.

"Seth will be at Auburn," I repeated.

Adam headed toward the truck, his fist balled as he walked.

"Adam."

"I don't want to hear it right now," he answered. "I'm already mad at you. Don't give me a reason to be madder."

"Well, if you're already mad, I might as well tell you every-thing, right? You can be mad at me all at one time." He contin-ued walking, so I sped up. "I knew Auburn was on his radar, but when I found out—"

"Hold up." Adam pivoted and looked at me so disgusted I wanted to cry. "How did you find out?"

"Because I've talked to him," I answered. "He texted me before Thanksgiving."

"You knew you were accepted *before* Thanksgiving! So this

whole time we've been talking about long-distance relationships, you knew you got in? You let me tell you how I felt about them without saying a damn word about getting accepted?"

"Would it have mattered?" I asked. "You had a pretty solid opinion of them, regardless of what I said."

"Too late to find out now, isn't it?"

I threw my hands up, so frustrated I could barely see straight. "I'm sorry, but I had enough I was dealing with. I've got a boyfriend I'm probably going to lose to football, an ex-boyfriend who won't quit texting me, scholarships, school, and a million things in between! Why would I tell you and make it worse?"

"How long has Seth been texting you?"

"That's all you heard?"

"How long?" Adam repeated.

"September."

"September?!" Adam took a step back, closing his eyes as he tilted his head toward the sky. "Why didn't you tell me?"

"I'm not texting him back. *He's* texting *me*. When he called while I was at the hospital, I told him—"

"You talked to him while you were at the hospital?!"

"He called me," I repeated.

Adam's jaw clenched as his head cocked to the side. "So let me get this straight. You've kept Seth a secret, you kept your admission to Auburn a secret, you told my grandma I needed to go to Alabama, and the whole time I thought you were being honest? Wow. Anything else you want to tell me? You and Seth getting back together when you get to Auburn?"

"No!" Adam tugged on the truck's door, but I pushed it closed. "We're not getting back together. I don't want Seth!"

"You obviously don't want me, either, since you chose to lie about everything."

"I haven't lied to you about everything."

"Okay, you didn't lie," he said. "You kept everything a secret, even after I let you in. Do you know how hard that was for me, or did you not care?"

"I care."

"Clearly." He leaned against the truck, crossing his arms as he stared at me. "How long did you know he planned on going to Auburn?"

I looked away. Adam was right. I did lie. I lied about everything.

"How long?" Adam repeated.

"We made an agreement last year," I answered. "Seth knew how much it meant to me to go there, so we agreed to go together. He wanted to go to Auburn. I wanted him to go to Auburn. That's changed."

"The pair of you agreed to go to Auburn together, and you never said anything? This is fucking perfect." Adam yanked the door open, and I moved out of his way. "I'm taking you home."

"Adam."

"I can't be around you right now."

I inhaled, trying to steady the world as it spun around me. "Don't do this," I pleaded.

"You did it, Claire. Not me."

"I didn't do anything!"

"You've been lying to me this whole time!"

I shook my head, tears streaming down my cheeks. "I didn't know how to tell you, and I was worried about what you'd say.

We aren't in an easy situation, Adam. We already disagree about college. We're already trying to figure that out, so the last thing I wanted to do was bring Seth into the mix."

"Then you should've trusted me, Claire. If you can't, why are we even doing this?"

"Because I love you."

"And I thought I loved you."

Survive

"Isn't there something better to look at?" Riley asked, frowning as we entered Senior Hall.

"No idea," I answered, "but I'm getting the same stupid looks."

I shot a narrowed gaze at a girl across the hall. She pretended to tie her shoes, oblivious to the lack of laces on her riding boots.

The week following my fight with Adam dragged at a snail's pace. Pader High was too small for me to avoid him. He was everywhere, pretending like I didn't exist while I tried to do the same. It was pointless, but it was the only option I had.

Riley had it worse. She and Tate were Pader High royalty. Their breakup was the biggest event of the year, and the most talked about topic on campus.

"Take a picture. It will last longer," she snapped, passing a crowd of football players gathered by the bathroom. She raked a hand through her hair and groaned. "I'm so over this. I'm over these people. I'm over this school. When do we graduate? The sooner I get to South Carolina, the better."

"Sixish months," I answered.

"Let the countdown begin."

She split off toward her locker, but I hesitated, transfixed on Adam, who was putting books in his locker with a girl at his side. She wore swoony eyes and was laughing too loud to be reasonable. It should've been me. Not too long ago, it was me.

"Want me to deck him?" Case asked, leaning against my locker. His brow was furrowed, and his eyes narrowed. My protective little brother had my back, yet again.

"I'm okay," I said.

"You sure? It can be a punch and run."

"He's faster than you. You wouldn't get very far."

I traded out my books, and Case waited, staring at Riley from where he stood. I caught his glances and sighed.

"Don't do it," I said, closing my locker.

"Don't do what?"

"Make a move."

I stepped away and he met my pace.

"I'm your older sister, so I'm required to tell you when you have a bad idea," I explained. "She's going to college in eight months, and you'll be here. Enjoy your time while you have it, and worry about girls after you're graduated." I turned, glancing at the library. "I need to stop in here before Mrs. Jenkins shuts the system down. Catch you after practice?"

"I'll grab a pizza," he replied. "We'll watch *Planes, Trains and Automobiles*."

"Sounds great."

Through the library's open doors, the lemony scent of furniture polish and the musty aroma of books hung in the air. Mrs. Jenkins, the librarian, stood behind the counter with a stack of books and a scanner in her hand. She nodded at me as I headed for the shelves.

"I'm checking these in," she said, motioning toward the stack, "but then I'm closing up. Try to hurry, please."

"Yes, ma'am."

I darted to the section on ancient Greece and pulled my notebook from my bag. I had a world history project due in a week, and I'd been too preoccupied to finish.

"Adam, we'll be closing in a minute," Mrs. Jenkins said. "Please find your selection as soon as possible."

"Sure thing."

My nerves stood on edge as I caught a glimpse of him out of the corner of my eye. He was headed in my direction, wearing his red-and-black letter jacket over a navy T-shirt and a fitted pair of jeans. He looked good, but Adam's looks weren't the problem.

"You working on history?" he asked, his voice low as he stopped beside me and grabbed a book from the shelf.

"Yeah. You?"

"Same." He flipped through the pages, then put the book back. "I've been too busy to get it done."

"Football?"

"Among other things." He chose another book and surveyed the writing on the back. "You haven't been around much," he said, shifting so he faced me.

"Neither have you," I answered.

I put the book back, but Adam took it as soon as it hit the shelf. Fine. Wasn't what I needed anyway. I took a step back, searching for a book on the top shelf. When I found what I was looking for, I tried to grab it, but it was too far out of reach.

"Sucks to be short," Adam said, grabbing the book. "Bet you wish you had a few more inches."

"Bet you wish that, too."

He chuckled and handed me the book, giving me the first real smile I'd seen since our fight. Even though we were broken up, that stupid smile tugged at my heartstrings.

"I need to go," I said, turning. "Thanks for the book."

I checked out while Adam searched the shelves. He lingered behind, but caught up as I exited the school's back doors.

"Hey," he said, slowing as I stopped beside my car.

I pushed the unlock button and glanced at him. His cheeks were tinged pink from the cold, and his hair was windblown.

"What do you need?" I asked, rubbing my arms to ward away the cold.

"My grandma's asking about you. It's been over a week. She misses you."

"I miss her, too."

Adam shifted the weight on his feet and scanned the empty parking lot. "Would you call her?" he asked, sighing. "She hasn't been doing well. It would do her some good to talk to you."

"I'll call her on my way home," I answered, nodding.

I paused as he met my gaze. There were so many things I wanted to say to him, but I couldn't do it. I couldn't find the words to tell him how sorry I was, and how much I still loved him.

"You doing okay?" I asked.

"I'm fine, but I've got to go." He turned, the gravel crunching beneath his feet as he walked to his truck.

We were far from good terms, but Wanda was an exception

to our conflict. If she needed me to call, I'd call. That would never change.

* * *

The hospital sent my call to Wanda's room the same time I entered my driveway. Outside, dressed in a thick Christmas sweater, my mom hauled a tote across the yard. The holidays were upon the Collins household; no light would be spared.

"Hello?" Wanda said.

"Wanda?"

"Claire!" In the background, her heart monitor beeped. She grumbled something about respiratory therapy, then returned to our call. "Sorry. That darn doctor is stuck on these three-a-day therapy sessions. Thinking about tossing the breathing thing in the hazardous materials bin. Think it'll keep him away?"

"Probably not," I answered, chuckling.

"Fine. Guess I'll deal with it." She coughed, heaving heavily. "You see," she sputtered. "All this therapy and still got this cough."

"It's for your own good."

"Now you sound like Adam." She paused, coughing again. "I'm glad you called. I need you to do me a favor. Waited a tad too long, and I'm afraid if I don't ask, it won't get done."

"What is it?"

"I need someone to get Adam a birthday gift from me."

My words hung in my throat. Hadn't Adam told her we broke up?

"His birthday is the fifth," she said. "I would do it myself, but I'm limited to the hospital gift store. The selection is a bit underwhelming. Nothing in there screams teenage boy, unless he's taken a sudden liking to stuffed animals and angel figurines."

"Wanda." I sighed, trying to figure out how to let her down gently.

"Oh! I bet I could order him a small cake. Maybe one of the bakeries would be willing to deliver to the hospital? What do you think, dear?"

"I think he'd like that."

"Fabulous! It would have to be sugar free, of course, given my dietary restrictions, but maybe we can spruce it up. I don't know. I'll think on the cake while you focus on the presents." She coughed again, this time longer than before.

"Wanda, are you okay?"

"Peachy," she answered, coughing. There was a brief pause, then she was back on the line. "There's some cash in the second drawer of my nightstand. Feel free to take whatever you need."

My mom knocked on my window, and I held up a hand to halt her. She ignored me and raised a tangled string of icicle lights.

"One minute," I mouthed.

"I wonder if they can do a sugar-free ganache!" Wanda continued. "Oh, chocolate truffles?! Tiramisu?"

"All of those sound great," I answered, "and I'll get him a gift. Don't know what it'll be, but you'll have something to give him."

"Thank you, dear. You're a real sweetheart."

"You're welcome." I glanced at my mom, who was now standing beside a ladder, this time scowling as she held a clump of tangled icicle lights. "Um, hey, I've got to go. My mom's decorating our house, and she's having an issue with the lights."

"Okay, hun. I'll see you soon?"

"Yes, ma'am."

I walked across the lawn, meeting my mom as she made progress untangling the lights.

"This looks fun," I said, "but I thought we were doing this after Friday, when Dad could help."

"He's distracted. Besides, I want the lights up sooner rather than later." She handed them to me and scooted the ladder across the grass. Dead leaves crunched beneath her feet. "And, since you brought it up . . ." she said, smiling.

"Friday's the championship. I know." I studied the candy-cane stakes strewn across the lawn. "Those new?" I asked, changing the topic.

"Yeah." She stepped off the ladder again. "Got them in the mail today, along with another box you'll love."

"A box of what?"

"If I told you, the surprise would be ruined." She hooked her arm around mine and led me toward the front door. "Now, I know you already have the mock version from Homecoming, but this is different."

"What's different?" I asked, following her into the house.

She entered the living room, beelining to a large cardboard box beside the couch. She squatted and pulled an object from inside, a piece of clothing wrapped in a clear plastic.

"Happy early Christmas," she said, handing it over.

The plastic clung to my fingers as I opened the gift. Inside was a black, bedazzled jersey with *Pader* written in large block letters on the front. The rhinestones sent rainbows over the walls, sparkling in the sunlight that poured through the living-room windows.

"What do you think?" she asked.

"It's beautiful."

I turned the jersey over and stared at Adam's number on the back. Emotion swelled in my throat. My mom didn't know about the breakup because I hadn't told her. It was easier to handle on my own.

"I love it," I said, forcing a smile. "Thank you."

"You're welcome."

She headed back to the front door, and I walked up the stairs, breathing in short spurts. By the time I made it to my room, my composure was gone. I pressed my back against the inside of the door and cried, letting go of all the emotions I couldn't keep buried.

This wasn't my first go-round with heartbreak. I knew what it was like to cry myself to sleep, to want someone I wasn't sure I was meant to have. I knew what it was like to wait on a phone call that never came and to hope the next day would be different. I knew what it felt like to have my heart returned to me in pieces, smashed by a guy I'd trusted more than I should.

Adam wasn't Seth, and this wasn't the same situation, but it still hurt. I missed Adam. I needed Adam. But sometimes life had its own plans.

I wasn't the Claire who'd moved to this town, but I was stronger for the hand I'd been dealt. Even if it took a while, even if it meant I repeated my mistakes, I would get through this, too.

I would survive Adam Meade.

Learn

"Thank goodness for youthful company! These old people are driving me nuts."

"Hello to you, too."

Wanda grinned as I closed the door behind me, cutting off the sound of the hospital staff.

"I can't stay long," I said, "but I come bearing gifts."

"I thought you were staying for Adam's birthday party," she answered. I shook my head, and she frowned. "Now, that just won't do. As a hostess, you're supposed to help serve cake and whatnot. Granted, the cake is far from perfect. I'm hoping he'll be too hungry to notice."

"I'm sure Adam will like it regardless." I handed her his birthday present, a large bag with printed balloons, different shades of tissue paper, and twirly ribbons wrapped around the handle. "Wasn't sure what to get him, but this was the best option."

"If he doesn't like it, he can get over it," she answered. She gave me back the present and I put it on the windowsill, where a bouquet of flowers sat. "Those are from your parents," she said, smiling. "The nurse brought them in yesterday. Said it was the most beautiful arrangement she'd ever seen. Tell them I said thank you, please."

"I will."

I took a seat on the couch and glanced at the Western on the TV. Wanda followed my gaze, but I felt her attention shift and looked at her again. Her green eyes were sunken into her pallid face, exaggerating the weight she'd lost while in the hospital. Gone was her perfectly curled hair. Gone were her rosy cheeks. Still, she smiled. Despite the battle she was waging, she still smiled.

"What?" I asked, grinning.

"I'm glad he found you."

My stomach knotted, and I swallowed hard, feeling the smile slide from my face. He still hadn't told her.

"Wanda—"

"Oh, I know," she said, waving me off. "He didn't have to say it, it's written on you both. I'm sorry I interfered."

I relaxed, releasing the breath caught in my chest. "It wasn't just about Alabama," I answered, shaking my head. "It was about everything—Auburn, long distance, my ex. I kept things from him. That's on me."

"Don't shoulder all the blame, dear. It takes more than one person to tango." She turned off the TV and let out a sigh. "I've been thinking a lot lately, cooped up here in this room. If I know one thing about my grandson, it's when he's torn. He's torn on what to do. The way you look, I can see you are, too."

"I think Adam's made up his mind," I replied.

"I think he puts up a good front," she answered.

She held up a hand, releasing a deep, hacking cough. I stood and grabbed a large cup from her tray. She took it willingly, her thin fingers enveloping my hand before I could retreat.

"Are you okay?" I asked.

"I will be," she answered. Her smile had softened, wearing sadness that wasn't there before. "I love my grandson," she said, looking at me. "He's the light of my life, one of the things I'm most proud of, but he's stubborn. He makes up his mind, sets out to do whatever it is he's doing, and doesn't think twice about whether he's on the right path or not. Now, I don't know who initiated this break of yours. I don't know the details, and I don't need to know the details. What I do know is he was the happiest he's been in a long time. You did that, Claire. You brought out parts of him I hadn't seen since before the accident, parts I was afraid he'd buried for good. You made him laugh, you made him smile, but most important, you made him *feel*. I know love when I see it, and that boy is still head over heels for you."

"I screwed up," I whispered, tears burning my eyes.

"Then learn from your mistakes," she said. "Learn from this experience, learn from all your experiences." She tilted her face into view as I swiped tears from my cheeks. "Life isn't about everything we do right, dear. It's about everything we do wrong. It's how we take our mistakes and use them to our advantage. Use what happened to make it right. I have faith you'll know what to do."

"What if I don't?" I answered. "What if I ruined us for good?"

"You didn't."

There was a knock on the door, and Wanda's respiratory therapist poked his head inside.

"You again," she said.

"Me again." She swore, and he stepped into the room. "Three times a day," he reminded her, grabbing an object from the shelf.

"Should've thrown that in the hazardous materials bin," she answered. She looked at me and frowned. "Looks like I've got a date with this guy, but remember what I said. Everything can be fixed. Let go of the stubbornness and find your way."

"And you think he'll forgive me?"

"I think he already has."

* * *

Wanda's words stuck with me. They replayed themselves over and over, cementing themselves in my mind.

Stadium lights illuminated BB&T Field, burning bright against the winter night. Thousands of people flocked there for North Carolina's 2A State Championship game. Everyone wanted their team to win.

"Did you talk to Adam?" my mom asked, her eyes scanning the field as a country singer finished an a cappella rendition of the national anthem. I shook my head, and she frowned. "I'm sure he's anxious," she said. "Your father was a bundle of nerves."

I focused my attention on the field and found Adam near the middle, black tape wrapped around his wrist and a black jersey with the same number as mine. I wanted to talk to him, but there was only one place his head needed to be—the game.

A whistle blew, and he tossed the football to one of the team's sports techs. He, Tate, and another guy participated in the coin toss, then jogged back to the sideline.

"You ready?" my mom asked, waving her foam finger as the team took the field.

"As ready as I'll ever be."

The first two quarters flew by in a blur of pass completions, yardage gained, and first downs. We went tit for tat with the opposition, equally matched in speed and strength.

As halftime approached, the other team was up by five, and no one on either side knew which team would take the title.

The time dwindled to zero. My dad and the guys left the field, and the marching bands took their place. Their musical compilations were broadcast over the intense PA system, and cheerleaders ran up and down the sidelines trying to keep the crowd's energy up. It was something to fill the break, but when the players finally exited the locker rooms and returned to the field, everyone was focused again.

The second half was a defensive battle. The opposition blocked our path to the end zone, and we kept them out of ours. It was a back-and-forth string of fourth downs, punts, and quarterback sacks, and it was easy to tell Adam was feeling the pain.

As the clock wound down in the last quarter, Tate received a punt deep in our own territory and ran it all the way back to the other team's forty-yard line. On the next play, Adam took the snap and shuffled back in the pocket, looking to pass as the receivers ran their routes downfield. They were too heavily covered.

He tucked the ball in his arms and ran it to the outside himself.

Bam!

Bodies collided and pads smashed together as Adam was tackled by a guy three times his size. Adam rolled onto his stomach and lay there for a minute.

My breath left me in a rush as a sickening feeling swept through my veins. Both sides of the bleachers grew eerily quiet as my dad and the trainer ran across the grass. When Adam stood, I finally felt like I could breathe. He was okay.

Second and six, 1:04 remaining

"Set. Red five. Red five. Set. Set. Hut!" Adam caught the ball and pitched it to the tailback, who shot through a gap and wasn't taken down until the twenty-yard line.

"Ladies and gentlemen," the announcer said, his voice deep. "There's a flag on the play. Unnecessary roughness, defense, number ninety-six, fifteen-yard penalty. Pader first down at the five-yard line."

First and goal, 0:56

"Black twenty-three. Hut!" The center snapped the ball, and Adam tucked it to his chest before shifting left and handing it off to a running back.

"Get in there," I urged, my voice a murmur among the crowd. "Get in there. Get in there."

He was stopped at the line of scrimmage. With both teams out of time-outs, the clock continued to count down.

Second and goal, 0:23 . . . 0:22 . . . 0:21 . . .

"Hut!" Adam received the ball and shuffled backward as a defensive tackle broke free and sprinted straight at him.

"Throw it!" I screamed. "Throw it!"

Adam ran from the tackle, searching for anyone to receive the ball, but he was sacked.

Third and goal, 0:08 . . . 0:07 . . . 0:06 . . .

Adam stood several yards back from the line and lifted his foot. The ball flew behind the center straight into his hands.

. . . **0:05 . . . 0:04 . . . 0:03 . . .**

Tate darted into the end zone, covered by a defensive back. He pivoted as Adam pulled the ball back, thrust his arm forward, and launched the ball in his direction.

. . . **0:02 . . . 0:01 . . .**

At the back of the end zone, Tate jumped, finding the ball in his gloved hands. He came down on top of the defensive back, with one foot in bounds on the red-and-black-painted grass.

"We won! We won!"

My mom wrapped me in a hug, tears streaming down her face. They did it. They were North Carolina 2A State Champs.

The bleachers emptied in a frenzy, with most of the people making their way to the field. My dad was waiting at the low wall, his arms outstretched for my mom. He pulled her into a tight hug, kissed her firmly, then hugged me. Beaming and covered in Gatorade, he was the happiest I'd ever seen him. He earned it.

My eyes scanned the crowd for Adam. He stood on the sideline, smiling as he talked with teammates. Eventually, there would be a time to seek him out. We'd talk about this victory, talk about everything else between us, and work out our issues. This wasn't the time. He deserved his glory.

I passed through a thick crowd of people, leaving him to his celebration. When I reached the edge of the field, though, I heard my name.

I turned, hearing my name again.

There were so many people, so many potential possibilities, but I saw him as he said my name a third time. My stomach knotted and nausea rose in my throat.

Standing along the fence, wearing a navy-and-gold letter jacket bearing a *B*, was Seth.

23

Mistakes

Anger, sadness, frustration, memories—everything fought each other in an instant.

I hadn't seen him since that day in Baker Heights when I'd stood on my porch and watched him walk away from me. Everything was broken—my relationship, my plans, me. He'd left without a thought, pretending like everything we ever had was irrelevant. And now he stood here, staring at me with the same intensity he always had.

He took a step forward, and I took one back, knocking into an elderly man who was passing through the crowd. The man stumbled, and I caught him, my cheeks flushing red.

"I'm so sorry," I said, helping him straighten. "I didn't see you there."

"No worries," he answered, winking as he adjusted his cane and continued on his way.

"Claire," Seth said again, his hand finding my shoulder.

I froze and my breath left me. I was too scared to turn around and face him and too pissed off to understand why he had his hand on me.

"Get your hand off me," I said.

He stepped around me, lowering his hand as he came into full view. His eyes were rich brown, full of caution and intrigue. His brown hair was shorter now, close cropped and gelled. He had scruff where he didn't before, a sharpness to his features, and a smile that should've knocked me off my feet.

"I'm sorry," he answered. I moved to step around him, and he blocked me. "I just want to talk," he said. "That's all I want to do."

"I don't want to talk to you." I tried to go again, and he blocked me. "Dammit, Seth. Go away! I don't want to see you. I thought I made that clear."

"And I'm still in love with you. I thought I made that clear."

I shook my head, trying not to deck him. "You don't get to come here and say that to me. You have no right to be here. This is *my* town. My home. My life. Get your own."

"Baker Heights isn't the same without you!" he answered. "I'm miserable there. I'm miserable every time I pass your old house, every time one of our songs comes on the radio. Do you know how many times I've wanted to skip school, find you, and never let go? I was an asshole, okay? But I want you back. I'll do whatever it takes."

"You're too late."

When I tried to walk past him, he grabbed my hand and pulled me back. I spun, landing a hand on his cheek. "Get your hands off me!" I yelled, yanking my hand away. "Or you'll get more than slapped next time."

Seth rubbed his cheek, his eyes narrowing in my direction. "You're a selfish bitch, you know that?"

"Yeah, but you're an arrogant prick who is too moronic to understand what the phrase *go away* means." I took a step back, not even caring we were making a scene. "You can't show up here, expecting me to forget everything that happened! *You* broke it off. You didn't want me. You wanted your freedom, and you wanted a fun senior year. Well, congratulations. Hope it was everything you expected it to be."

"This wasn't what I wanted."

"And crying in my room all summer wasn't what I wanted, either, but it happened, and I dealt with it. I survived. So will you."

Seth's lips spread into a thin line, his expression resolved to the truth. We were done. End of story. Nothing he said or did would ever change what he broke, and for the first time it looked like he understood.

"I'm sorry for what I did," he said, putting more distance between us. "If I could go back and do it again, it would've been different."

"Then learn from your mistake. I did."

He surveyed me quietly, neither of us moving as people walked by. "You will always be the first girl I ever loved."

"I'll be the one that got away," I answered.

He turned, disappearing into the crowd that slowly exited the stadium. Once he was out of sight, relief flooded through me. Our conversation was about more than Seth, more than his flaws or how he made me feel. This was about me, realizing what I deserved and what I wanted.

I wanted Adam.

The crowd on the field had thinned, making it easier to navigate. I found Adam talking to Tate in the end zone, laughing together like they always did. He looked at me over Tate's shoulders, then nodded my way. When Tate turned, it took him point two seconds to split off and move to a different group.

"He could've stayed," I said, stopping in front of Adam.

"You looked like a woman on a mission. Didn't want him to get caught in the shrapnel," Adam answered. He pushed sweaty hair from his brow, the dark strands staying plastered to his skin despite the effort. "So what's up? You want an autograph?"

"Tempting, but no. I wanted to see if we could talk tomorrow."

"We can talk now."

"No," I answered, shaking my head. "This is your night. Go enjoy it. Tomorrow. Lunch?"

"Can't tomorrow. I have to go to the hospital." He shifted the weight on his feet, his brows tugging together. "Something's wrong. You okay?"

"No."

"Then we'll talk now."

He held out his hand, and I took it, following him toward a multistory structure on the other side of the field. It was quieter there, where the chaos and excitement of the stadium hadn't quite reached. He stopped and leaned against a metal railing, studying me with intent.

"What's going on?" he asked.

"Seth was here."

He straightened and craned his head toward the field, but I squeezed his hand to regain his attention.

"He's gone," I said. "But I knew after I talked to him that I couldn't just sit around pretending like this is okay. It's not. None of this is okay."

I closed my eyes, letting out a shaky breath as I tried to find the words.

"I'm not perfect," I said. "I'm irrational, I'm emotional, and when Seth started texting me, I was conflicted. That relationship didn't end well, so when I moved here, all I wanted to do was finish this year, get out, and go to Auburn. I thought it would be easy. Then you came in and wrecked everything."

"*I* wrecked everything?" he said, crossing his arms.

"Yes. You're a pest, Adam. You pester me, taunt me, and frustrate the crap out of me. Half the time I can't stand you, and the other half the time you're deliberately trying to make me mad. You push my buttons on purpose. I swear it's your favorite pastime. And when you aren't pushing my buttons, you're nagging me. You could literally give an intro class on how to piss off Claire Collins."

"Then you should've—"

"And I love it," I said, shaking my head. "I love when I'm in the halls, and we're standing at my locker, talking about our days. I love when I'm in class and you're behind me, nagging me for the millionth time."

"Claire—"

"I love how when I'm stressed, you know exactly what to say to make it better. And I love that you know me. I love that you always know how to make me smile. I love that you can walk in a room and my day is instantly better. I love your quirks, your sense of humor, and your wit. I love everything about you."

"Claire."

"And I'm sorry for hurting you," I said, holding his gaze. "I'm sorry for losing your trust, and for not appreciating you when I had the chance. But I'm not sorry for loving you. I will never be sorry for—"

Adam kissed me, his mouth slanting over mine so unexpectedly that it took me a second to understand.

"I forgive you," he whispered, pushing his forehead against mine. "Because I miss nagging you. I miss pushing your buttons. I miss the way your nose crinkles when I tell a joke that isn't funny, and that you laugh anyway. I miss your smile. I miss the way it feels to hug you, and how much I hate letting you go. I miss everything about you. And I love you, too."

My arms wrapped around his waist as his hands cupped my face.

"And I know we still have college to deal with," he said, "but we'll make long distance work. Not an ideal situation, but at least I get you."

"You're up for long distance?"

"I'm in, if you're in."

I kissed him again and smiled. "Meade, you've got yourself a deal."

The End

I stared at the cap and gown hanging in my closet. The black satin robe was draped across a plastic hanger with a summer dress beside it and my heels on the floor. Downstairs, my mom's voice carried. There was excitement in her tone, despite her occasional glimmer of tears.

"Ten minutes!" I hollered, grabbing my clothes.

The fabric was itchy against my bare arms, and I scratched them as I walked down the steps. My mom stood below, her phone pointed in my direction as she snapped pictures. "Mark!" she yelled. "We've got to go."

"I'm coming," he answered, adjusting his tie as he entered the foyer. He lifted hazel eyes to the stairs, and his face smoothed with pride, making me want to cry. "You look wonderful," he commented. Then, staring at my mom, he added,

"But she's running late, too. Want to blame someone? Blame your daughter."

"Way to kill the sentimental moment," I answered. My mom pulled me into a hug as Case entered through the front door, grinning. "What's wrong with your face?" I teased.

He scowled. "It's your graduation day. Don't make me be mean to you."

My dad waved the keys, passing my brother on his way out the door. "I'm the one headed to the car," he said, looking at my mom. "Remember this the next time you get onto me for being late."

We pulled up to Pader's stadium, anxiety running rampant. My parents found their seats in the bleachers, while I trudged across the field. My heels dug into the grass as I looked for Adam, Riley, and Tate. I found the last two chatting with a group of people near the entrance to the field. Adam was nowhere in sight.

"I like those shoes!" Riley greeted, pulling me in for a hug.

"I like your haircut," I answered. "When did that happen?"

"This morning."

She slid her cap off and tousled the curls. A long strand of white yarn lay balled inside the cap, safety-pinned to the fabric.

I took it in my fingers and looked at her, confused. "Why is this in here?"

"Because I want to keep my cap." She tugged the string and smiled. "When we throw them in the air, all I have to do is hold the string. Problem solved."

"Did you see this on the Internet?" I asked.

"No. I came up with it all on my own." She smiled and carefully put the cap back on.

I glanced at Tate as he crammed his phone in his pocket. "Any word on Adam? Haven't heard from him since this morning, and I don't see him anywhere."

"Nope," Tate answered, glancing around the field. "He should be here somewhere. If I had to bet, he's probably talking to Mr. Acua. It's his last chance to hit Adam up for Alabama season passes."

"It's his own fault for mentioning it in class," Riley said. "If he wouldn't go around bragging about his team, he wouldn't have a problem."

"Says the girl who told everyone she's the University of South Carolina's newest cheerleader," Tate replied. He slung his arm around her shoulder and grinned. "When you do great things, you have to flaunt it."

"Is that why you've been purchasing UNC T-shirts by the dozen?" she asked.

"I have to represent."

A whistle blew, and Mrs. Jenkins crossed the grass, smiling as she neared. "Okay, ladies and gentlemen. Let's get in order! We're starting in five minutes."

"You sure Adam's here?" I asked, scouring the field.

"He's here," Tate replied.

I would be seated with the top ten percent of the class. Riley, Adam, and Tate would sit alphabetically behind me. We lined up according to our seating arrangement, and "Pomp and Circumstance" played through the speakers as we crossed the field.

The warm sun beat down on us, burning its way through my sleeves. I tried to listen to the ramblings of my teachers and administrators, their words meant to be inspiring and insightful. Instead, I looked behind me for Adam.

He smiled at me as he straightened his cap and relaxed in his chair. Relieved, I turned around and tried to focus on the final moments of my high school career.

"Claire Elizabeth Collins."

My heels dug into the ground as I made my way to the stairs. I didn't want to fall in front of the entire town. Luckily, I didn't. With the rolled-up, cardboard-covered diploma in hand, I made my way back to my seat. I sat quietly as more names were called.

"Riley Madison Cross."

Riley made her way up the stairs, her hand gripping the metal rail. She was almost to the top when her cap flew off. White yarn floated along the breeze, covering the stage where she was supposed to walk. I heard Tate cracking up in his seat, and she laughed, scooting along unfazed while our principal waited to hand her the diploma.

When she reached her chair, she leaned forward. "It worked!" she whispered.

"It worked," I agreed.

We waited, quiet, while the rest of our class made their way across the stage. Adam was near the middle. His applause was arguably louder than the rest of the graduates', though I suspected my family and Riley's and Tate's were to blame.

After our principal thanked the crowd for their attendance, after the caps were thrown in the air and my high school experience was officially over, I found him. He gave me a quick kiss and bopped me on the head with his diploma.

"Thought you weren't going to make it," I said.

"Almost didn't. They're doing construction between here and

Charlotte. If my grandma hadn't made me leave when she did, I would've missed it."

I cocked an eyebrow as my parents approached us, Case in tow. My mom looked teary eyed, but my dad was brandishing a cell phone. He was more embarrassing than my mom.

"Here we have two graduates of Pader High," he said, ducking in closer. "Names, GPAs, future aspirations?"

"Oh, look at you!" Wanda said, her face visible on his phone screen. "You look all grown up!"

"She's going to start crying, too," Adam whispered in my ear.

Sure enough, Wanda got just as teary eyed as my mom. It disappeared soon enough, when she turned her attention from the screen and glanced at someone in her hospital room.

"Ready for respiratory therapy?" a guy asked.

Her eyes narrowed. "You again?"

"Yes. Three times a day."

FaceTime ended halfway through her griping at the therapist.

"You two planning to celebrate, or should I whip up a home-cooked meal?" my mom asked, hugging me. "Adam, I know how much you enjoyed my lasagna the other day." Case gagged behind her, and she nudged him. "You hush, Case Michael!"

"We're fine!" I said. "Appreciate the thought, but Tate's grilling."

"Okay. Call me if you need a DD," she replied.

"Better yet, call me," Case said.

She swatted him on the shoulder with her clutch, and they exited through the crowd, leaving me with the good-byes and congratulations of my classmates. My senior year was the furthest thing from what I expected, but it was done. Auburn awaited.

* * *

Smoke hung in a clearing, hovering above our bonfire as flames extended toward the sky. I stayed by the fire and sipped from a red plastic cup. Mosquitoes landed on my legs, and I swatted them, sloshing my soda on the ground.

"Hey, sweetheart." The fire crackled loudly as two strong arms wrapped around me. "What's a pretty girl like you doing out here by yourself? Better question: Where's your boyfriend? If you're single, can I have your digits?"

"Always such a charmer, Meade."

"I try." He kissed my neck and released me, his hand finding my free one. "Where are Riley and Tate?"

"Playing hide-and-go-seek," I answered. "They wanted to know if we were interested, but I passed."

"Good choice. Now I can steal you away without Riley protesting." There was a mischievous glint in his eyes, and I grinned as he pulled me across the grass.

"You aren't going to get me in trouble, are you?"

"Why? You want me to get you in trouble?" When I shook my head, he shrugged. "Fine, be the responsible one."

"I'm a stick-in-the-mud. I own it."

He opened his truck's passenger door and motioned inside. After we were both inside, he pulled away from Tate's barn and took the dirt road to the back of the property.

We continued down that road for a while, surrounded by

trees. Eventually, the trees thinned into an open space, the sky breathtaking above.

He pulled off the road and parked.

"What are we doing?" I asked.

"Currently, getting out of the truck." He unbuckled his seat belt and pushed open the door to the warm June air. "You coming?"

"Yeah."

I unhitched my seat belt and stepped into the night. Adam pulled a flashlight from beneath his back seat and handed it to me. Then he tugged a pair of blankets off the seat and tossed them in the bed of the truck.

"If I didn't know you better, I'd think you planned this," I said.

"Well, yeah." He shut the door and moved to the tailgate. It opened with a thud, and he grabbed both sides of my waist to hoist me up. "I've been planning this little getaway for the last twenty minutes."

"Impressive."

"I'm awesome. You can thank me later."

I stood in the bed of the truck and situated the blankets against the metal. Once I was done, Adam joined me. He relaxed against the cab, and I cuddled up to him, a soft breeze riffling my hair as he glanced at the sky.

"I can't believe high school's over," he said, sighing. "It feels like everything else took forever, but this year flew by." I looked at him, and he lowered his gaze, a small smile gracing his face. "Except for prom week. That lasted too long."

"You looked good in that tux. Suits do you well, Meade."

"Yeah, yeah. I'm gorgeous. I know."

"And arrogant."

"And you like it."

He kissed me and shifted against the metal, his arm loosely draping over my shoulders. I nestled against his chest, soaking in his scent and relishing his touch. We would head to college soon, but the University of Alabama was only three hours from me. We could make this work. This would work.

"Tell me what you're thinking," he said, his chin coming to rest on the crown of my head. "You're being quiet. You're never quiet."

"You think we can do this?" I asked, lifting my gaze. "You, me, long distance, college?"

"It's not going to be easy," he answered. "I think there's going to be many nights where I randomly show up at your dorm because I miss you, or where you get a pair of football tickets emailed to you as a hint to come watch me play."

"Ooh, someone's clingy."

"I own it," he said, grinning. "But I know we're going to get through this. You're going to kick butt in Auburn's Honor's College, and I'm going to get a national championship. We'll see each other on the weekends, and it'll be like nothing ever changed."

"I think you're right."

"I'm always right." He leaned back, his eyes still on me. "And one day we'll be sitting in this very same truck, talking about our plans for after college. We'll look back at everything we went through, every year that passed, every stupid argument, everything that should have torn us apart and didn't, and I'll still feel the same. I don't care where we're at or what we're doing, as long as I have you."

I kissed him, his warmth radiating through me as we sat beneath the North Carolina sky. I didn't know what the next chapter held, or the challenges we'd face, but we could handle it. We would always survive.

Acknowledgments

When I wrote *Surviving Adam Meade*, getting published was a far-fetched dream from a small-town girl. There were so many people who helped me get here. Without your love and support, this wouldn't be possible.

To Kat and the entire Swoon Reads team, thank you for taking a chance on Claire and Adam. You've taught me so much about the publishing process, and pushed me beyond what I thought myself capable. Working with you has been amazing. Jessika, Melinda, and Danielle, I'm so glad we were chosen together. Thank you for being there for me, for anything and everything. You are incredible! Katy, the best mentor I could've asked for, thank you for the million questions you've answered. Thank you for guiding me through this process, and for being so patient with me along the way. And to the readers, I could never tell you how grateful I am for your unending support. Thank you for all your votes and comments, and for going on this journey with me. You're the best!

To Allen, my inspiration in so many ways, you never saw writing as a dream I couldn't achieve. You listened to me talk about these character for years, answered every football question I asked, and refused to let me give up. You've been there every step of the way, my guide and my confidant. Thank you for being my best friend. Thank you for the sacrifices you made so I could do this. I love you more than words could ever express. To my little ones, I hope this inspires you to go after your dreams. I will love you until the end of time.

To my mom and dad, words could never thank you for everything you've given me. Mom, you were always my biggest fan. You never let me shy away from my goals, even when I thought they were impossible. Thank you for encouraging me to share this passion with the world, and for reading all those first drafts without complaint. Dad, the bravest man I've ever known, it's no coincidence that Claire's dad has your humor. I love you so much and carry you with me always. I can't wait to tell you about this someday. And to the rest of my family, especially my brothers, thank you for making life fun.

To Ashley, Laurel, Kylie, and Dionn, I'm so lucky I got to do high school with you! Thank you for the sports trips, Friday night football games, UIL events, moments spent goofing off in class, and summers I could never forget. I will cherish those memories forever. To the families of those four ladies, thank you for treating me like I was one of your own. You made Post feel like home.

And to the people of that small West Texas town, your guidance and influence got me here. Thank you for making me fall in love with football as only you could, and for giving me such an amazing place to finish school. Post will always hold a special place in my heart.

Check out more books chosen for publication by readers like you.

DID YOU KNOW...

readers like you helped to get this book published?

Join our book-obsessed community and help us discover awesome new writing talent.

1

Write it.
Share your original YA manuscript.

2

Read it.
Discover bright new bookish talent.

3

Share it.
Discuss, rate, and share your faves.

4

Love it.
Help us publish the books you love.

Share your own manuscript or dive between the pages at **swoonreads.com** or by downloading the **Swoon Reads app.**